Poetic Injustice

by

I0451905

Alicia Dean

Poetic Injustice

COPYRIGHT © 2008 by Alicia Dean

Cover Art by *Nicola Martinez*

The Wild Rose Press
PO Box 708
Adams Basin, NY 14410-0706
Visit us at www.thewildrosepress.com

Publishing History
First Crimson Rose Edition, 2008
Print ISBN 1-60154-337-9

Published in the United States of America

Dedication

For my father, Dean Robertson, who taught me the love of baseball and so much more. I still miss you.

Chapter One

The crimson-black stain spread from the woman's head wound and ended unevenly in the center of her blonde hair. It would almost look as if she'd been interrupted in the midst of a bad dye job, except she was lying face down, leaching more of the dark blood into the supple leather of the cream-colored sofa.

Detective Samantha Colby bent closer, trying to see the victim's face without touching the body. She couldn't. Nor could she see signs of any other injuries. Not that any were needed. The bloody gavel lying on the floor next to the corpse had been more than sufficient.

Sam rose and blew out a breath, resisting the urge to remove her jacket. The heat was oppressive, unusual for Cincinnati, even in July. The sweltering temperatures magnified the smell of decay, not something one would expect to encounter in a five million-dollar mansion. CSI techs wandered in and out of the room, cameras flashing, baggies opening and closing as evidence was neatly secured.

Sam's olive shell, minus the navy blazer, would be much cooler attire, but it would probably show her armpit stains. It wasn't the image a 'together' homicide detective should present.

She turned to the uniform, Walburn, and said, "Got an ID on the vic?"

His eyes glittered with excitement. "It's not confirmed, but the house belongs to Mona Morrison." He watched Sam expectantly.

"Mona Morrison?" Sam lifted a brow.

"You know, Judge Mona."

She'd heard of Judge Mona, although she'd never watched her program. Judge Mona was a television judge who tried 'real' cases in front of millions of people.

Great. If the dead woman turned out to be Judge Mona Morrison, this was going to be one of those high profile cases with the captain demanding it be solved yesterday.

Sam's partner, Frank Torino, peered over her shoulder at the victim. Frank was a stout man with dark, wavy hair and a booming voice he couldn't bring down to a respectable level, even at a death scene. He wore a fishing hat and a Hawaiian print shirt with a design almost as loud as his voice.

Frank removed the ever-present drinking straw from his mouth and squinted at Sam. "Shit, Spike. We'll have our hands full with this one. You ever watch her show?"

Frank had a nickname for everyone. Sam's was Spike because he said she was like a bulldog. When she got something in her teeth, she wouldn't let go.

She shook her head. "Don't watch much television."

"She's a tough broad. Real man-eater. I'd bet my right nut the doer is male."

"Wouldn't advise it," Sam said dryly. "You lost your left nut in our last bet. Don't want to be completely nutless."

"Smartass," he mumbled, only his mumble was more like a roar. He shook his head and grinned, chucking Walburn on the shoulder. "See, she's got a sharp tongue. That's why she can't keep a man."

Sam's face heated and a quick band of hurt squeezed her heart. She forced a chuckle, but it sounded hollow and phony.

It wasn't that she couldn't *keep* a man, it was just that she had extremely poor judgment in choosing them. So, she'd stopped trying and began concentrating on her job.

Frank met her eyes and the smile slipped from his face. "Ah, geez, Spike. I'm sorry. I didn't mean anything by it."

"It's okay, Frank."

She looked back at the corpse and felt guilty for her childish hurt feelings. This woman's life had come to a frightful, brutal end. A slap to the ego was insignificant compared to that.

"Is the ME here yet?" Sam asked Walburn.

"He's on his way."

As if on cue, the low din of a motorcycle sounded, growing louder until it drowned out the buzz of the blow flies and the clicking and chatter of the CSI techs and detectives.

Surely, he hadn't... Sam clenched her jaw in irritation.

She stalked to the front door and stepped outside, ostensibly to greet the pathologist, but in truth, she was anxious to breathe a few precious molecules of air that was only slightly tainted with the stench of death.

Sam walked to the bottom of the steps and crossed her arms over her chest as she watched the ME, Doctor Dexter Hawkins, dismount from his motorcycle.

Dexter Hawkins had been the county's Medical Examiner for two weeks. He'd transferred to Cincinnati from Boston, and Sam had only met him once. Something about him had irritated her then, but that couldn't compare to the agitation she felt now.

Even his good looks and charm grated on her. His tall frame moved with an easy grace, sort of a swagger/stalking motion, like that of a jungle cat. Green-blue eyes crinkled at the corners and the dark stubble covering his jaw wasn't quite thick enough to conceal the dimples slashed in each cheekbone. He was the kind of good-looking that was just too obvious, the kind that made you know to stay away, as if a big red stop sign were embedded in his skull.

He slid his helmet off and walked toward Sam. He wore a black, button-up shirt tucked into well-worn Levis and his longish, dark blonde hair was tousled from the ride.

"Hey, Detective," he said, giving a flash of white teeth as he stopped at the bottom of the steps.

Sam's lips tightened. For God's sake, the least he could have done was shave. "Doctor," she returned primly.

"You look kinda pale. If I didn't know better, I'd swear *your* body was the one I was here to examine."

Although his eyes never left her face, it felt as though they raked her from head to toe. If they had, she was sure he'd have found her lacking in comparison to the voluptuous, empty-headed types he no doubt dated. Sam wasn't sure why she was stereotyping him like that, but it made her feel marginally better to do so.

Ignoring his comment, Sam said, "Do you really think a motorcycle is appropriate transportation to a death scene, Dr. Hawkins?"

He turned and glanced at the bike, his arm making a sweeping gesture toward it. When he looked at her again, his eyebrows were raised, his expression that of someone who'd just heard a joke, or was speaking to a dim-witted child. "That's a Harley."

Sam let her lips curl into a contemptuous smile. "Sorry. I'd forgotten how sensitive boys can be about their toys. Do you think a *Harley* is appropriate

4

transportation to a death scene?"

He stepped closer, until they were almost nose to nose, even though Sam stood three steps above him. She was fairly tall for a woman, just over 5'7, but Dexter Hawkins towered over her, his broad shoulders making his 6'4 height even more intimidating.

Sam flinched, and then went still, as if that would keep him from noticing she smelled like sweat and death. It didn't keep her from noticing he smelled of fresh air, some manly, musky soap, and mint.

"The only women I strive to please," he said softly, "are my mother and my sexual partners. So far, you're neither."

She flushed and took a step back, telling herself it was less a sign of retreat as an aversion to having her space invaded. The movement made her a few inches taller than him since it brought her to a higher step. It helped to restore a modicum of control of the situation.

Lifting her chin, she stared down her nose at him, aware of news crews and onlookers watching the exchange. There were several things she wanted to say, but discretion ruled, so she turned her back on him and headed up the steps.

She heard him chuckle softly behind her. "You know, you might be a little more comfortable if you took off that jacket and unclenched your butt cheeks."

Sam stopped and whirled, almost bumping into him. Fury oozed forth like the sweat that leaked from her pores. His expression was one of challenge and amusement. At that moment, even though she barely knew him, she hated him. She choked back her response, refusing to let him bait her in front of half the city.

He peered up at her and she was acutely aware of the fact that her makeup had probably melted and her dark hair must be plastered to her head with sweat.

Great, just how she wanted to appear for the cameras...not to mention Hawkins' eagle-eyed attention.

"You know," he said thoughtfully, "when we first met, I thought your eyes were brown. But out here in the sunlight, they're more of a mahogany with a hint of black cherry. I also didn't notice the freckles sprinkled across your nose." He smiled. "Cute."

If her face could warm any further, it did at that moment. She wasn't sure of his intentions, but it seemed like he was making fun of her. Clenching her teeth, she snapped, "Let's not forget that my nose is slightly crooked and my chin is too pointed and my eyes are too far apart."

He shook his head. "Flaws are what make a person unique, make their features more interesting. You're a very attractive woman."

Momentarily disconcerted, she met his eyes, losing her breath for a split second.

He's testing you, playing you...ignore him.

Releasing an agitated sigh, she said, "This isn't exactly the time or place for flattery, Doctor Hawkins. Please follow me."

She turned and he followed her inside without further comment. She led him to the body and he pulled on latex gloves, squatting next to the corpse.

After a few moments, he rolled the victim over and gave a low whistle. "Wow, Judge Mona."

"You recognize her?"

"Yeah, I've seen her show."

That was pretty much an I.D. Yep. *Definitely* a high profile case.

"We knew this was her home, but we weren't positive she was the vic since she's lying face down."

"No doubt about it." He continued the exam. "Rigor mortis has begun to set in. Hard to pinpoint the time of death, but I'd say it was sometime before midnight last night."

Sam was reluctantly impressed with the air of professionalism he now displayed. "Can you be a little more specific?"

He shook his head. "Not right now. Once I do the autopsy, I can narrow it down some, but probably can't get exact. Maybe within a few hours. I'll check stomach contents, body temp, things like that. Then, with the data your people gather about how she spent her last hours, we can come up with a fairly close time of death."

"We're talking to neighbors now, then we'll branch out to friends and family. I'd like to attend the autopsy, by the way."

He straightened and slipped off the gloves. "Okay. I'll probably do the autopsy in the next two or three days. I have a few ahead of this one."

Playing the captain's tirade in her mind, Sam said, "Can you move it up? This will be a priority, considering she's a celebrity."

"I understand, but the other cases I have are just as important to me."

His sensitivity conversely annoyed her, even more than his nonchalance had. "I agree, Doctor, but the chief and the mayor—"

"Can wait," he interrupted. "I'll call you when the autopsy's scheduled."

She didn't respond, although there were several responses clamoring for release. Yes, most definitely, she did *not* like this man one bit.

Alicia Dean

Chapter Two

Shortly after Dexter Hawkins left, Mona Morrison's housekeeper, Eileen, arrived.

She was short and Irish with red-gray hair and hazel eyes that kept brimming with tears as she spoke.

"I come in late on Fridays, that's why I'm just now getting here. I had no idea. Oh, Lord in heaven, what a tragic, tragic thing." The woman twisted her plump hands together and shook her head. "Who found her?"

Sam hesitated. Actually, the gardener noticed the stench and called 911. The first responders found her. Sam didn't want to give the disturbing details to the woman, though.

"We received a 911 call because neighbors were concerned and an officer found her." Little white lie, but less upsetting than the truth. "When was the last time you saw Miss Morrison?" Sam asked gently.

Frank handed the woman a glass of water and she sipped it, her brows drawn together in thought. They were sitting in the library which, in the enormous house, was far enough away from the place the body was found so as not to upset the housekeeper too greatly.

"It would have been yesterday evening. Thursday. Just before I left."

"Did everything seem okay? Was she worried or distracted in any way that you could tell?"

Her expression darkened. "She was agitated as usual when that scoundrel was around."

"Scoundrel?"

"That boyfriend of hers. They had a terrible row that night. Not that different from most nights, though."

"What's his name?"

"Calvin Rollins," Eileen provided promptly and with some satisfaction. "He's the one you should be lookin' for. He was always after her money and when she wouldn't fork it over, acted like a child who didn't get his way. Terrible."

Sam met Frank's eyes over the woman's head and they exchanged a knowing look. The 'significant other' was always a good place to start. A great percentage of murders were committed by boyfriends, girlfriends, or spouses. Sort of contradicted the studies in *Cosmo* magazine that determined being in love contributed to longevity.

"So, they fought last night?" Sam prompted. "Do you know what it was about?"

Eileen shook her head. "Not exactly. Always about one of two things, though. Money or other women. He fooled around on her, took her money. Too lazy to earn his own. Thought he was too pretty to have to, you ask me."

"Do you happen to know where he lives?" Frank asked, pulling the straw from his mouth.

"Don't know, don't care to." She crossed her arms under her breasts. "He's no good, you ask me."

So, Sam thought, *I'm guessing you don't care much for Mr. Rollins.*

Sam stood and handed the woman her card. "If there's anything else you can think of, please give us a call."

Eileen remained seated and looked around the room, a fresh wave of tears pouring from her eyes. "What'll I do now? I've worked for Miss Morrison for ten years. She was awful good to me. I don't know what to do next."

Sam placed her hand on the woman's shoulder and squeezed. "I'm so sorry. I know this is difficult. Just give yourself some time. You'll figure it out."

Eileen nodded, unconvinced, staring into the empty fireplace as Sam and Frank let themselves out.

****

He tugged the baseball cap lower, nearly covering his eyes, then wondered if he should have. Did it make him look suspicious?

He glanced around at the crowd standing just outside the gate. Neighbors, reporters, curious gawkers, all wondering exactly what had happened in the judge's home. He was the only person in the world—the only *living* person—who knew the truth.

His clothing clung to him with the damp heat of perspiration. Strange that—even with the nearly hundred-degree temperature—he felt so cold. He shoved his hands in the pockets of his pants to hide their trembling.

He couldn't believe he'd actually done it. But he had. They'd argued first. She was her usual acid-tongued, imperious self and that made it easier for him to do what needed to be done—had sealed her fate.

The memories would most likely haunt his dreams for the rest of his life, providing he could ever sleep again. He'd tried to sleep last night, after the murder, but every time he closed his eyes, he relived it.

He'd arrived unannounced at her door and confronted her. As soon as she whirled to stalk away from him, he swung the gavel, putting all of his strength into the blow. There was a loud *thwack,* like the sound of a watermelon bursting open. The impact traveled through his arms, vibrating through his muscles until he was momentarily paralyzed.

For one horrifying moment, he was afraid the blow hadn't been enough and he'd have to hit her again. But he knew he couldn't.

He started to freak out, nearly fainting with the enormity of what he'd done. If she didn't die from the first strike, he was screwed. She would call the police, he'd be arrested for attempted murder, and the bitch would live on. Because there was just *no way* he could bring himself to hit her again.

His worries were unfounded because she dropped, face-first, and lay motionless. The back of her head looked like an overripe tomato, and he knew she was finished.

Standing here now, in the reality of broad daylight, he still couldn't believe he'd done it. He thought maybe it had been a dream. A horrifying, unbelievable, never-happen-in-real-life, dream. After all, he wasn't a killer.

He closed his eyes, then snapped them open because he couldn't stand the images that appeared behind his closed lids. His stomach clenched and a wave of nausea swam upward, climbing into his throat. Clamping a hand over his mouth, he pushed through the crowd and stumbled to a row of hedges lining the sidewalk.

Now this *might look suspicious*, he thought, as he puked violently into the bushes.

****

Mona Morrison's assistant, Giselle Corinthia, was a stunning black woman with almond-shaped, topaz-colored eyes and perfect, straight white teeth that looked like they should be in an ad for responsible orthodontia care.

Mona's bailiff, aptly nicknamed Moose, was close to seven feet tall. His bulk seemed to want to break free from the putty-colored uniform he wore. Tears streamed down his broad, flat face and his giant shoulders shook with sobs.

Giselle gave him a look that was part sympathy, part annoyance, then turned to Sam. "What can I help you with, Detective?"

They were seated in a reception area, Giselle perched daintily on the edge of the burgundy and emerald green striped sofa. Moose sat like a large clay lump in the adjacent chair.

Sam pulled out a notebook, her gaze taking in both of them. "Do either of you know of any enemies Judge Morrison may have had? Anyone who might want to harm her?"

The two of them shook their heads, although Moose didn't look at Sam as he did so.

"Is there anyone you know of who argued with her lately?" Sam continued. "Someone who might have been angry with her?"

Giselle smiled. "Half of America was angry with her. She could be a bit harsh. But angry enough to kill her? I highly doubt it. Win or lose, the people on her show are paid and go home happy."

"What about people other than those on her show? Anyone she may have had a disagreement with? Especially recently?" Sam looked at Moose, who hadn't spoken, even though his snuffles had been a constant during the interview. "Would either of you know of anyone?"

Moose didn't reply, but Giselle said, "Mona and her boyfriend fought a lot." She sighed and shook her head. "Ironic how she continuously admonished the guests on her show for letting people take advantage of them, yet Calvin made a fool of her over and over, and she just took it."

The boyfriend again. Sam was anxious to speak with the elusive Mr. Rollins, but hadn't been able to reach him since Morrison's body had been found yesterday. Rollins wasn't home when she stopped by, and his roommate couldn't tell her where to find him. He wasn't employed, so she couldn't very well track him down at work. For now, she'd concentrate on other leads, but she wasn't giving up on lover boy.

"Anyone else you know of?" Sam asked.

"She also had frequent disagreements with our station manager, Carson Clayton."

"Where can I find Mr. Clayton?"

"He's out of town."

"Was he out of town the night of the murder?"

Giselle shook her head. "He just left this morning and he's due back Friday."

"I'd like to take some of the show tapes with me. Specifically ones where the litigants were especially volatile."

"I'm sorry," Giselle said. "I'm not allowed to let them out of the building. Unless you get a warrant," she added helpfully.

Sam nodded, trying to hide her frustration. She knew she could get a warrant, but she wanted to view those tapes immediately. "I'll do that."

"If you'd like, we can watch some now. I mean, it's not like I have a lot to do these days." A small, sad smile touched her lips. "It might be better, anyway, because I could answer any questions you have."

"Sure, thanks. That would be great."

Giselle led Sam to a small room with a large screen on one wall and various electronic equipment on the table next to it.

"I'll begin with some of the more recent, heated ones," Giselle said as she manipulated several buttons.

The screen lit up, then the opening credits of the program came on, showing Mona Morrison, very much alive and in different 'judicial' poses. Her pale blonde hair was pulled back in a tight bun, and although Sam knew she was close to sixty, she was youthful looking, even with her stern countenance.

On the screen, Moose stood next to the bench. After giving his spiel, beginning with 'all rise' and ending with the introduction of 'the honorable Judge Mona,' he folded his massive arms and commanded, "You may be seated." This persona was quite a contrast to the blubbering mess Sam had encountered a few moments ago.

The first case was a woman suing her ex-husband for bail money. He'd been arrested for domestic violence he'd committed against her, then had the nerve to call her to post his bond.

"Why did you call her to bail you out?" the judge demanded.

"Because, I didn't know who else to call," he replied peevishly. "I mean, we were married for fifteen years, have children together. I figured it was the least she could do."

"Even after you'd physically assaulted her?"

He shrugged. "I lost my temper. I didn't mean anything by it."

"Judge, he broke my jaw," the wife cut in.

Mona Morrison looked at the woman, then swiveled her reproving glare to the ex-husband. "My question is, *why* did you want out of jail?"

He looked at her incredulously. "Because it was awful. There were all kinds of criminals in there. Hell, I was terrified."

A gleam of satisfaction came into Mona's eyes and her voice rose. "Just as, I imagine, your wife was when you beat her, Mr. Jamison. I don't feel one bit sorry for you and you owe this poor woman the bail money. I wish she'd sued you for emotional damages, because I'd have granted her the maximum amount allowed. You're a low life, sir, and I can only hope that one day you encounter someone who'll teach you the lesson you deserve. In the meantime, pay the woman."

She banged her gavel and rose, but the defendant wasn't finished. "You can't do that!" he screamed, his face mottled with anger. "This bitch deserved it. You don't know what she's put me through!"

Giselle explained that the expletives had been bleeped out before the show aired, but they were viewing the uncut version.

On the screen, Moose seized Jamison's arm. "Out, sir."

Livid, the man tried to break free, but he couldn't budge Moose's hold. Sam thought she saw a flinch of pain on his face, then he went still. Mona gave him one more stern look, lightly tinged with triumph, and left the courtroom.

The next case was also a woman suing her ex-husband and Sam wondered if these types of cases were the most common, or if Giselle was showing more of these because they were the ones that most frequently became violent.

A blonde, attractive woman with large breasts was suing her ex for taxes he was supposed to pay in the divorce settlement.

The defendant, Keith Brahern, had brought his best friend and his brother as witnesses. When the best friend took his turn at the mic, he told the judge about all the hell the wife had put his friend through during the marriage.

"What does that have to do with the case, Mr. Avery? If you can't contribute information that's pertinent, I'd suggest you sit down and keep your mouth shut." Her tone grew louder and more strident with the last words and the man's face tightened.

"You don't have to talk to people like that," he said, still standing. "I was—"

"Sit down, sir, before I have you removed from my court."

"What the hell? You can't treat me—" He started toward the bench and Moose moved to intercept him. "Let me go, she's a fucking bitch! She doesn't know what the hell she's talking about. She's just like—"

The remainder of his tirade was cut off as Moose jostled him out of the courtroom, returning in seconds, looking nonplussed.

"Why don't you feel you should pay your share, Mr. Brahern?" Mona's laser stare impaled the defendant.

"I wasn't the one who wanted the divorce in the first place. It's not fair."

"What you want is not the issue, sir. The law is the law. Don't be such a sissy, whiny little mama's boy. Grow up and be a man."

Brahern's face paled and his fists clenched on top of the defendant's table. He didn't respond, but his eyes deadened, as if a light went out.

The brother sat behind him, not moving. It was as if the two of them were frozen. Sam wondered if she'd missed something, wasn't sure why they suddenly looked like hot air balloons that had been shot with a missile.

"If there's nothing further, I'll make my ruling after examining these documents." Judge Mona stood and exited the courtroom, her billowing black robes sweeping behind her.

She returned moments later, after what would be aired as a commercial break, Sam surmised. Somehow not surprisingly, Judge Mona banged her gavel and said, "Judgment for the plaintiff."

When the episode was over, Giselle said, "This actually turned out to be the worst one of all."

"Why's that?"

"Mr. Brahern, the ex-husband, committed suicide not long after it aired."

Sam drew in a quick breath. "Suicide? Because of the show?"

Giselle shrugged. "We don't really know, but that's why Mona and Carson had such a terrible fight a few days ago. She didn't want him to air it, out of respect for the family, but he insisted. He said it was good for ratings." She gave a grim smile. "Whatever sells, you know?"

Sam nodded, her mind filing away the information. She had a gut feeling there was something relevant here but wasn't sure exactly what. After all, Keith Brahern couldn't be their killer, he was dead. But the friend...

Before Sam could finish the thought, her cell vibrated. It was the Coroner's office. The autopsy was scheduled for tomorrow.

Chapter Three

Sam had been dreading the autopsy since she'd received the call. She hated attending, but it was a necessary part of her job. She didn't observe them all, but certain cases demanded she put herself through the unpleasant task.

Years ago, just moments into her first autopsy, she'd thrown up all over the ME's Salvatore Ferragamo oxfords. He'd attempted patience and understanding, but she could tell he was pissed. The scarlet that suffused his face and the tick in his left eye had been dead giveaways.

On one hand, she'd felt bad, on the other, she wondered what kind of idiot wore five-hundred-dollar shoes to cut up a dead body.

That had been fifteen years and countless autopsies ago. While she couldn't say she liked them now, she could say she hadn't thrown up since. Felt like it, yes, actually done it, no.

When Sam and Frank arrived at the morgue, the attendant, a young man with cornrows and mocha-colored skin, instructed them on how to suit up.

Once they were attired in gowns, shoe covers, gloves, masks, and goggles, he led them into the autopsy suite, where the body was laid out on the stainless steel table. A body block had been placed underneath the corpse, raising her chest and making her head loll back.

"Good afternoon, Detectives," Hawkins said, his words muffled by the mask.

She and Frank returned his greeting, and Sam noticed that, behind the goggles, Hawkins' eyes were missing their usual mischievous glint. He seemed respectful, subdued. It wasn't what she'd anticipated. She'd half expected him to be wearing leather, blaring *Born to be Wild* on the stereo, and preparing to cut open the cadaver with a switchblade.

Sam braced herself as Hawkins made the Y incision with a scalpel and peeled back the chest wall. An odor like raw meat wafted through the air and Sam swallowed against the bile filling her throat. She moved her gaze to Mona Morrison's face, not able to directly watch as he removed the organs.

The woman's skin was gray and waxen. On television, she seemed powerful and invincible. But lying here, silent...exposed, she didn't seem powerful at all. She seemed small, helpless, tragically victimized.

Alone.

Sam felt an unexpected wave of sorrow.

"Are you okay?"

She lifted her head at the softly spoken words and it was only then that she realized her hands were shaking. Hawkins' gaze was filled with concern and it made Sam want to shed the tears that were inexplicably crowding her throat, pushing back the nausea lodged there.

She nodded. "I'm fine."

He nodded slightly in return and continued, using a bone cutter to open the rib cage, then removing the chest plate, exposing the heart and lungs.

"This part always makes me want to hurl," Frank said, his voice sounding thin and watery.

Sam didn't respond, still close to tears without knowing why. She'd only cried once on the job in her entire career. It had been during a case where a routine drug bust had led to the discovery of a dead child. The little girl had been five years old and the daughter of one of the suspects. She'd been beaten to death and left in a back room for several days.

Sam had lost it, sobbing uncontrollably, so affected by the tragic loss of the innocent child, that she hadn't even felt embarrassed about her show of weakness.

Puke once, bawl once. It was as if her system had a built in maximum on displays of emotional weakness in the line of duty. She'd met her quota on both.

One explanation for her emotional state would probably be today's date. It was her and her ex's anniversary. Not their wedding anniversary, but the anniversary of the day he walked out on her three years ago. After six years of marriage, suspicions of his infidelity, and never quite feeling like she lived up to his expectations, he'd confirmed that theory by telling her that she bored him and he couldn't take it anymore. Then, he left. Before his motorcycle took him completely out of town, he cleaned out her bank account.

Hawkins emptied the cadaver's stomach contents, then began itemizing what he found. "Looks like whatever she had for dinner was mostly digested. I'd put the time of death at my earlier assessment, just before midnight on Thursday."

As the autopsy wound to a close, Sam asked, "Is there any indication of trauma, other than the head injury?"

Hawkins shook his head. "The cause of death was a cerebral hemorrhage due to head trauma. This would be consistent with the gavel found at the scene. I'd say that's your murder weapon, Detectives."

They'd discovered the gavel didn't belong to Mona Morrison. The killer had brought it with him.

"Thanks, Doc," Frank said. "You find anything else, you'll let us know?"

"I should have my report done by the end of the week."

Sam thanked him and followed Frank out the door of the morgue and into the fresh air, as anxious to escape the atmosphere of death as her partner.

****

Sam lived in a third floor apartment in downtown Cincinnati, convenient to the police department, which was where she spent most of her time. The apartment was a two-bedroom with a large living room that dwarfed her meager furniture—a plaid couch, matching recliner, and a 27-inch television.

The thing she loved most about living here was the view of the Ohio river and Great American Ball Park.

Her dad had retired last year after working in the front office of the Reds' organization for forty years. As a kid, Sam had gone to most of the Reds' games with him. Once in a while, her brother would come along, but not often. He didn't care much for baseball and that drove their dad crazy. At fourteen, Samantha discovered boys and didn't go as often after that. In retrospect, she should have stuck with baseball.

Sam shrugged off her blazer and put an Elvis Presley CD on the stereo, then grabbed a can of Diet Coke from the fridge and spread the case notes out on the table.

She studied the meager information they'd collected, wondering if the killer could be someone as unlikely as one of the litigants. It was insane. These court shows were on daily. At least three or four different judges were doing the same thing Mona Morrison had done. Surely Mona hadn't made one of the litigants angry enough to commit murder.

Because Sam didn't have anything else to go on, and because in this crazy world, anything was possible, she jotted down the names of the litigants in the episodes she'd watched at the station. There were the Brahern brothers, their friend, Avery, and the abusive husband with the domestic violence charge. She also added Mona Morrison's boyfriend, Calvin Rollins. Sam would look up their addresses and go talk to them, unless she landed a miracle solid lead first thing in the morning.

The station manager was a person of interest, but Sam found that unlikely, too. He and the judge had been arguing for years, although the blow-up about the man who committed suicide had apparently been a doozie. Mona was his bread and butter. Sam couldn't imagine him offing her over something like that.

She was going through her notes for the second time when her mother called.

"Just wanted you to know that Landon stopped by with the kids and we wish you were here. We miss you, you know."

Ah, brother Landon and his dutiful Sunday visits. Her mother was *so* lucky to have a son like him.

"I know, Mom, I'm sorry. It's been really crazy at work."

"Sure it has, hon. You have a very important job and I wouldn't want to take you away from it. I just wish I could see you a little more often. You wouldn't believe the way your nieces and nephews have grown. Makes me realize how I'm not getting any younger. I'd hoped to have a few more grandchildren by now."

Sam nearly groaned aloud. Over the years, her mother had systematically, with love and kindness, instilled a tremendous amount of guilt in her. Guilt that her only daughter was divorced and childless at thirty-three.

"Well, guess that wasn't in the cards for me, Mom."

"You know, it's not too late, dear. Your biological clock is ticking away, I'll admit, but there's still time."

Time, but not the opportunity and not the desire, Sam thought, but didn't say it. It was easier to just agree. Go along to get along. "I know. Maybe I'll meet someone soon."

"You're not seeing anyone right now?"

"No." Rather than make excuses for her lack of a love life, Sam decided to end the call. "I'm kind of in the middle of something. It was great talking to you, Mom, love you. Give Landon and the kids and Dad my love, too."

With her mother muttering a hasty, flustered goodbye, Sam hung up the phone. She opened the freezer, perusing the dozen frozen dinners neatly stacked with the label facing out so she could quickly choose between beef tips and noodles, cheese enchiladas, fettuccini alfredo, meatloaf, and so forth.

None of them appealed to her, but she chose the meatloaf and stuck it in the microwave.

Just as the timer dinged, the phone rang again. She didn't recognize the number on the caller ID but picked it up anyway.

"Samantha? This is Dexter Hawkins."

Hearing his voice was so unexpected, its timbre so warmly masculine, she felt a rush of heat tingle through her. She squeezed her thighs tightly together to make it go away. "Hello, Dr. Hawkins. What can I do for you?"

"The station gave me your number. I hope I'm not disturbing you."

"You're not," she said, but he was. Just not in the way he meant.

Sam traded her Diet Coke for a Tecate and went to stare out the window, the phone pressed to her ear. Bright sparks of blues, whites, reds and greens lit the sky over the river. Fireworks were going off at the ballpark, which meant one of their guys had hit a homerun.

"I was calling to make sure you're okay," Dexter said. "You know, after today."

"I'm fine, thanks. It's always difficult, no matter how many times."

"Tell me about it," he agreed sympathetically.

She was touched by his empathy. Autopsies couldn't possibly affect him the way they did her or he wouldn't do it for a living, yet he was trying to make her feel like less of a weakling. She felt another warm rush, except this was one of gratitude, and something else she wasn't willing to scrutinize too closely. After all, she didn't like the guy, did she?

"Find out any more from the autopsy?" she asked for lack of anything else to say, and for fear of getting on a personal topic with him.

"Not yet. I'll keep you posted."

"Thanks."

Silence settled between them. Sam couldn't think of anything to talk about, but was strangely reluctant to let him go.

Finally, she said, "I appreciate you calling to check on me. I'll talk to you soon."

"Okay. Goodnight, Samantha."

She hung up the phone, then took a long pull from the Tecate, trying to ignore the glow his call had left her with.

Sighing, she re-heated the frozen dinner, then sat at the dining table. As she ate, she went over the case files once more, making a supreme effort to concentrate on them instead of on the quagmire of her feelings for Dexter Hawkins.

Poetic Injustice

Chapter Four

The next morning, Samantha went to the Greater Cincinnati Mall where Keith Brahern's ex-wife worked at a cosmetics store.

Sam envied Krista Brahern's flawless skin, but comforted herself by concluding it was most likely due to her expertly applied makeup. Muted blue eye shadow complemented her eye color, and bright coral lip gloss shimmered on her lips. She looked a little older than she had on television, and the breasts looked even larger.

Sam introduced herself and showed her badge. "I'd like to ask you a few questions about your ex."

Krista's impeccably arched brows lifted. "My ex? It *was* suicide, wasn't it?"

"Yes. Well, as far as I know. That's not why I'm here. It's about Mona Morrison."

"I heard. That's crazy. You think it had something to do with Keith?"

"We don't know. We're just following up on even the smallest lead. Your ex-husband took a beating in the courtroom. He and his witnesses seemed a little upset, especially his friend."

Krista nodded. "Yes, but Eric's just like that. He's a hothead, likes to be the center of attention.

25

Keith and Todd were upset, but not murderously so."
She smiled. "They were satisfied because Keith's tax
debt was taken care of and they were each paid to be
on the show."

"But your ex-husband committed suicide shortly
after the program aired. Do you know why he killed
himself?"

"Not exactly." Her voice lowered, turned gloomy.
"Keith was always a bit unstable. I told myself it had
nothing to do with me since we'd been divorced for
five years, but then again, I wonder. It was a messy,
horrible divorce." She took a tissue from a box on the
counter and dabbed at her eyes, giving a wan smile.
"Almost as messy and horrible as our marriage. I
sometimes wonder if my taking him to court stirred
up all those feelings again."

A thin, middle-aged woman and a teenage girl
with a nose ring and spiked hair came in then, and
Krista excused herself to take care of her customers.

Sam waited patiently, watching as Krista
opened a case of eye shadows and the young girl took
a ridiculously long time to choose two ridiculously
overpriced pallets.

Once they had conducted their business, they
left and Krista came back over to Sam. "Sorry about
that. We'll probably start to get busy here in a few
minutes. Was there more you wanted to ask?"

"Yes, but I'll be brief so you can get back to
work. Did your ex leave a suicide note?"

"I heard he did, but I can't say for sure. His
sister is the only one in his family who still talks to
me, and we're not exactly best friends. We've never
spoken of the suicide. It's just too painful for her."
She lifted one shoulder apologetically. "So, I really
don't know about a note."

Sam nodded. "Did your ex-husband's friend or
his brother display any violent tendencies that you
were aware of?"

Krista thought for a moment, then shook her

head. "No. Like I said, Eric was hot-tempered, but it was more about yelling and getting red-faced. I never knew of him hurting anyone."

Sam consulted her notes. "I think that's all I have. I appreciate your cooperation." She handed Krista a card. "If you think of anything else, please give me a call at one of these numbers."

Another customer, a lone woman this time, entered the store and Sam left, wondering why an innocuous incident such as the mild annoyance Keith Brahern exhibited on Judge Mona's show gave her such a strong gut feeling it had something to do with her murder.

****

By noon the next day, no one had come running into the station to confess, and Sam still hadn't been able to reach Calvin Rollins, so she went to see Todd Brahern while Frank checked out the list of merchants where gavels were sold.

The insurance office where Todd worked as a salesman was located in a business district in the north area of Cincinnati. Sam entered through the glass door where a twenty-something, very pregnant girl with friendly but homely features sat at the front desk.

"Can I help you?" The receptionist smiled, deepening the reddish freckles that were a few shades darker than her hair.

"I'm here to see Todd Brahern." Sam lifted the detective shield hanging around her neck so the girl could read it.

"Is he expecting you?"

"No. I didn't make an appointment."

"Well, I'm sure it won't be a problem. Hold on a sec." She lifted the phone and hit a button. "Mr. Brahern, there's a police detective out here to see you. Can I send her in?"

She hung up the phone, then beamed up at Sam. Placing her palms on the desk, she grunted and started to heave her bulky frame to a standing position. The girl would be plump, even without being pregnant, but now her protruding belly was so large and tight, she looked like she could pop any time. "Right this way."

"Don't get up," Sam said, but the girl was already on her feet.

"It's okay. I need to walk. I'm almost a week overdue and I'm hoping I can convince this little guy to show up soon."

"A week overdue and you're still working?" Sam asked in astonishment and admiration.

She nodded as she led Sam to a glass-encased office. "My husband and I need the money. Besides, I like my job. Mr. Brahern is a doll to work for."

They stopped by a closed door, and she turned the knob, pushing inward. "Go right in."

"Thanks," Sam said. The receptionist gave her another smile before waddling back to her desk.

Todd Brahern stood to greet Samantha. He looked the same as he had on television, but his manner was much more pleasant.

He shook Sam's hand after she introduced herself, then indicated the brown leather chair facing his desk. "Please, sit down."

Sam took a seat, slipping her notepad from her jacket pocket. As she did, her fingers touched the other objects in the pocket and she sighed longingly. A lighter and one cigarette. She carried them as a talisman that she would solve the case soon. Each time she successfully closed an investigation, she would celebrate by smoking one, and only one, cigarette. Until two years ago, she'd smoked regularly. Now she only infrequently allowed herself the guilty pleasure.

"Thank you for seeing me, Mr. Brahern. I know this will be difficult for you, but I have some questions I need to ask about your brother."

A sadness entered his eyes and he nodded

slowly. "Please, feel free. But I can't imagine what you would need to know about my brother."

"This is in reference to the Judge Mona murder investigation. I'm sure you're aware she was found dead?"

"Yes, yes, of course." He shook his head and made a tsk tsk sound. "Such a shock, a tragedy. But what could my brother possibly have to do with that? He's been...deceased" he stumbled over the word, his voice lowering slightly as he said it, "for over a month."

"We're just following up on some of the cases that came before the judge. Even the tiniest lead can sometimes help us catch the person responsible."

"Of course, I know that from watching Law and Order." He smiled. "What can I help you with?"

"Your brother's friend, Eric Avery, seemed pretty livid about Judge Morrison's treatment of your brother."

"Eric was a bit temperamental. I never understood why he and Keith were so close."

"You said 'was'. Mr. Avery isn't..."

"Oh, no." Brahern vigorously shook his head. "He moved out of state shortly after the court date. He's out of our lives, good riddance, so I think of him in the past tense."

Sam felt a slight deflation at the news that Avery lived out of state. For some reason she couldn't name just yet, she liked Avery for the murder, but if he were out of state at the time, it pretty much cleared him.

As if reading her thoughts, Brahern said, "He's been in town the past week or so, visiting friends. But I heard he left to go back to Dallas yesterday."

So, Avery had been in town at the time of the murder. Could still be something there. But why move out of state, wait several weeks, then come back and murder someone who had humiliated your best friend? Especially someone famous, who would be hard to get to. That would take a lot of planning. And for the planning, the killer would most likely need to be in close proximity of the neighborhood for a good length of time.

"Do you and your ex sister-in-law get along?" Sam asked.

"She's not my favorite person, but I hold no ill will toward her. I don't blame the divorce or Todd's death on her. But, I wish she could have, I don't know, loved him enough or something to help him."

"How angry were you and your brother with Mona Morrison after the show?"

Brahern shrugged. "Not angry at all. He was a little embarrassed. Kind of pissed that his ex-wife won, but he owed her the money, so it was the right decision. I thought the judge was a little too cruel, but anyone who's seen her show knows what to expect." He shrugged again. "I certainly didn't blame that for his suicide. My brother was quite emotional and very irresponsible. We had a difficult childhood and while I pretty much overcame it, put it behind me, he never did. He would sink into these gloomy moods, almost depression, and nothing could rouse him from them. I guess in one of them, he was so down, he decided to end it."

"Your ex sister-in-law mentioned that there might be a suicide note?"

He shook his head. "No, no note. I wish there had been." Moisture glistened in his eyes. "Then, maybe I'd know for sure. Know if there was something I could have done."

Sam let an uncomfortable moment pass, before offering lamely, "I'm sure there's nothing you could have done."

Often in the course of doing her job, she found herself giving comfort, spouting platitudes to grieving loved ones she'd never met before. Fact was, her words weren't always true. Maybe there *was* something he could have done. How the hell did she know?

Brahern slowly nodded but his mind didn't seem to be on her words. He was far away, maybe with his deceased brother.

"If more questions come up," she told him as she stood. "I'll be in touch."

He nodded and wiped the tears from his eyes, shaking her hand before she left.

Sam was amazed at how affable and accommodating he'd been. How genuine. She wondered if he truly knew nothing of Judge Mona's murder, or if he were just that good at subterfuge.

Chapter Five

That evening, Captain Betancourt called Sam into his office for an update on the murder investigation. The captain was in his mid fifties, thin, with sallow cheeks and a receding hairline. His small stature made him act more aggressively than necessary, as though he had something to prove. Once you got past his blustering, he was a decent man. He and Sam had worked together since her rookie days, and they had an easy, comfortable rapport.

"We need to talk to Eric Avery," Sam told him.

"Who's he?"

"The best friend of the defendant from the Judge Mona show. The defendant who committed suicide."

"Okay." Betancourt spread his hands in a 'what's the problem' gesture. "So talk to him."

"He lives in Dallas."

"Then, he's not your suspect."

"But he was in town at the time of the murder."

Betancourt leaned back in his chair and linked his hands on top of his head. "You know expenditures such as that have to be approved. And I can tell you, you're going to have a hard time getting that one through. It's pretty far-fetched that the friend of a defendant on a TV court show would murder the judge. Do you have any idea how many of those shows are on? How many cases there are, day after day? How many winners and losers?"

Sam huffed a breath and nodded. "I know. It's a long shot, but there's something about this situation that's pulling at me. I can't put my finger on it."

"Well, put your finger on your phone keys and call the guy in Dallas. We'll worry about a trip if the evidence suggests it would be productive."

"Okay, fine."

"The media's all over this one, Colby. You got anything I can tell them?"

Yeah, go fuck themselves, she thought. Aloud, she said, "We're on it day and night, Captain. We just don't have much right now."

"Any other suspects? Evidence?"

She grimaced. "We've got enough suspects to start our own boy band, but not enough evidence to cover your bald spot."

He scowled and unlinked his hands, running his fingers across his thinning hair. Ignoring her jibe, he said, "You better come up with something soon. The chief's breathing down my neck. You know what they say about shit running downhill. You're getting ready to be covered in it."

"I know, I know." Sam sighed. "Trust me, I want it solved as badly as you do. Maybe more so."

"You solve this one, it will be quite a feather in your cap. Help further an already bright future. High profile case like this, you solve it quickly and..."

And she would possibly make rank. A buzz of excitement shot through her. She tried not to dwell on that aspect of her job, but she had to admit, a promotion would be a dream come true. *Sergeant* Samantha Colby. She liked the sound of it.

"You'll be at the party Saturday, right?"

"Party?"

"Geez, Colby, sometimes I wonder if you listen to

anything I say. The chief is giving the mayor a party for his sixtieth birthday. If you don't want a huge blight on your bid for sergeant, you'll be there."

Sam nodded. She didn't want that, but she really didn't want to attend the stuffy function, either. Sighing, she left the captain's office.

Frank was sitting with one hip on her desk, a straw protruding from his lips. He looked up when she approached. "Your buddy, Evil Kneivel, may be getting himself in some trouble."

He was referring to Hawkins and called him 'Evil Kneivel' because of the motorcycle.

"Why's that?" Sam asked, shooing him off her desk and sitting in her chair.

"He's messing with Conniver's old lady."

Anthony Conniver was a detective in Narcotics. Sam felt a twinge of...not jealousy exactly, more disappointment. Just when she was beginning to think Hawkins might be an okay guy, she learned something like this.

The feeling was followed quickly by a sense of validation. She could spot 'em a mile away. Her radar had been honed to razor perfection when it came to bad boys. Well, good thing she found out now, before...

Before what? She barely knew him. It wasn't like they were on the verge of a relationship.

She was saved from a response by another detective, Jonas Cummings. "Colby, someone here to see you."

Jonas brought a man to Sam's desk and she looked up into the greenest eyes she'd ever seen. Of course, they may have looked so green because of contacts, or because the man was so tanned he'd make George Hamilton look pasty.

The guy was drop-dead gorgeous in a metrosexual, look-at-me-aren't-I-pretty, sort of way. Sam guessed him at around twenty-five, but figured if he didn't stay out of the tanning booths, he'd look fifty in another five years.

"This is the judge's ex," Jonas said, and left the Abercrombie model at Sam's desk.

Calvin Rollins smiled, his even white teeth looking like high beams in his tanned face. "Vin Rollins," he said, extending his hand.

Sam gave it a brief shake. *Vin* must be a little more hip than Calvin. "Thank you for coming in, Mr. Rollins. You're a difficult man to find."

"Always on the go. But, when I heard a beautiful woman was looking for me, I came running."

Not commenting on his lame attempt at flirtation, Sam invited him to sit in the chair next to her desk.

"What can I do for you, Detective?" he asked as he dropped into the chair.

"You can tell me where you were on Thursday night."

His waxed brows drew together. "I was at Bonger's. You know it? It's a club over on forty-fifth. Maybe me and you could grab a drink there sometime."

"What about earlier that evening?" Sam said, ignoring his invitation. "You were at Mona Morrison's home, weren't you?"

His eyes drifted away before settling back on her. "Yeah, so what?"

"I understand you and Judge Morrison had a disagreement that evening. Mind telling me what that was about?"

"Do I need a lawyer?"

"That's up to you. I'm just interviewing you at the moment. You're not under arrest."

He nodded. "I needed a few bucks and she refused. We had words, she threw me out."

"Did it get physical?"

He smiled, angling toward Sam, his arm resting on her desk. "Never, baby. I'm a lover, not a fighter. Go out with me and I'll show you."

Sam let out a long breath and looked him in the eye. Leaning so close she could see the glint of his contacts, she spoke softly. "Listen, Calvin, you're a little young for my tastes, and your charm is wasted on me. I'd be willing to bet you've got more money than I do, so you're not really gaining anything here. All you're going to do is annoy me and work harder than you're used to, so let's drop the come-on act and answer my questions, before I change my mind about the arrest thing."

He blinked rapidly a few times, then shrugged and sat back. "Sorry, habit."

"What time did you leave Ms Morrison's house that night?"

"I think it was around eight. I was meeting some people. I could tell I wasn't going to get anywhere with Mona so I decided to let her cool off and try again tomorrow. But, there wasn't a 'tomorrow'. She's dead." He sighed, looking pained, but his grief seemed more about him than her.

"Any ideas who might want to kill her?"

"Not really. Unless it was something to do with drugs."

Sam lifted her brows. "Drugs?"

He nodded, giving her a smug grin. "She was a doper. Maybe a dealer, or someone she was doing coke with, got pissed and did her."

Sam sat back, stunned. She never would have dreamed that Mona Morrison was a drug user. Not the woman she'd seen on those tapes. Not the crusader for right and wrong. But, then again, anything was possible. Some of the most upstanding citizens hid deep, dark secrets. Or, this asshole could be lying.

Sam wanted it not to be true. Even though she hadn't watched her show when Mona Morrison was alive, Sam admired what she had seen of her in those few episodes Giselle had shown her. Sam wanted to believe that the woman she saw on those tapes—tough, moral, uncompromising—was the real Judge Mona. That in this society of no accountability, there were still people out there who believed there were consequences for your actions and no bad deed should go unpunished.

Sam asked Rollins a few more questions, then told him he was free to go.

After he left, Sam called the ME's office for Dr. Hawkins. The woman who answered the phone said he wasn't in, so Sam asked for his assistant.

"He was called out on some personal emergency. Can I help you with something?"

"I have some questions about Mona Morrison's autopsy."

"No, sorry, can't help you there. You'll have to speak to one of them."

"Can you tell me when Dr. Hawkins will be in?"

"Don't know, probably tomorrow. He coaches a baseball team and he's at the field with them now. You want to call his cell?"

Coaching a baseball practice? On a day when he had a high profile murder case in his workload?

That, along with the tidbit about the married woman, sealed Sam's image of him. He was a loser, all right.

She shook her head and jotted down the number, then dialed it after disconnecting from the morgue. No answer. Of course not, he was playing *baseball*.

She nearly growled with frustration as she grabbed her keys and headed to the door.

****

The Impala's charcoal gray interior was like an oven...an oven that was sitting in the middle of a desert...a desert that was located in hell.

Sam slipped off her blazer—even its light linen cloth was too much clothing for the sweltering heat inside the car. She took her sunglasses from the console and slipped them on, then jerked them off

37

when they practically melded to her flesh, something she should have anticipated since they'd been cooking inside the car for hours. She held them in front of the barely cooling air vents until they wouldn't sear the skin on her face and slid them back on.

She drove to the ball field, spotting Hawkins as soon as she pulled into the parking lot. There were four fields, but two of them were empty. Little leaguers played on one field and teen boys played on the other. Hawkins was with the older team, boys who looked to be fifteen or sixteen. He was tossing balls up and hitting them to the kids in the outfield.

Sam slipped her jacket back on over her white shell, wishing she hadn't when she opened the door and the furnace outside blasted into the cool interior of the car.

As she approached, she heard Hawkins yell to a boy who'd just missed a grounder. "Glove in the dirt, Peterson, you learn that crap in little league. Remember, whoever misses the most balls wears a skirt to next practice."

"Don't say that, coach," said a short boy standing near second base. "Tremaine'll start missing balls on purpose."

"Bite me!" came a shout from the outfield, most likely Tremaine. "I bet you miss *your* balls since the operation."

A burst of laughter and good-natured ribbing ended abruptly when the boys, seemingly all at once, noticed Sam.

Hawkins turned and saw her, then stood immobile for a few seconds before gesturing to one of the boys shagging balls the fielders threw back in. The boy took over batting to his teammates while Hawkins jogged over to Sam.

He wore a white muscle shirt, gray athletic shorts, and a black Red Sox ball cap. He stopped in front of Sam, the tendons in his arms gleaming with perspiration as he crossed them over his chest. He gave her a lopsided grin, his eyes sparkling in the afternoon sun. "What a nice surprise."

Thoughts of how cool and comfortable he looked, how hot and miserably wilting she felt, and the news about his screwing around with a married woman combined to make her response a little sharper than necessary. "Well, since you weren't in your office on a work day, and I needed to speak with you, I had no choice but to track you down."

"Is it a crime to take a day off, Detective?"

She shook her head irritably. "Not a crime, but a little irresponsible to take a day off work to *play*."

"To play? The boys..." He looked behind him toward the field, then swung his gaze back to her. He seemed about to say something, then he shook his head. "Never mind. What can I do for you?" His jaw tightened, causing the dimples to deepen.

"Did you do toxicology testing on Mona Morrison?"

"Yes. But the results aren't back yet. Why?"

"One of the interviews uncovered a claim of drug abuse. Cocaine."

"Cocaine? Judge Mona?"

Sam shrugged. "I agree, doesn't sound likely, but you never know. If it's true, it could have played a part in her murder."

"Toxicology results can take six to eight weeks."

Sam blew a breath out between pursed lips. "I don't have that long. I need some answers right away."

"We can do a hair analysis. That will show if there is cocaine in the system."

"How long will that take?"

"Normally twenty-four to seventy-two hours after it reaches the lab. I'll go in tonight and take the samples and send them out. I'll ask them to put a rush on it and let you know when I have the results."

"Thank you," Sam said, trying to sound a little

more cordial than she had earlier.

"Sure. And look, I'm sorry I wasn't available at the office. Sorry you had to come all this way."

She didn't respond right away. His apology made her feel like an ass. A strand of damp hair had come loose from her ponytail and she tucked it behind her ear. She could feel sweat trickling down her sides, underneath the jacket. Damn heat. "No, I'm sorry," she sighed. "This heat makes me a little crabby."

He grinned again, one of those charming grins that reached his eyes, making them glint like sunlight on an aqua sea. "It's okay." He reached out and took her lapel in his hand, letting the material slide between his thumb and forefinger. "You wouldn't be so hot if you took this off."

Sam's chest tightened and her breath slowed. The back of his hand hadn't actually stroked her breast, but it had come close. "That won't help," she said, her voice sounding raspy and unnatural.

"No?"

She shook her head. "Maybe if you moved back, I wouldn't be so hot."

His mouth crooked in amusement. "Oh? I make you hot?"

Sam's face flushed even warmer. "Of course not, I mean, not like that. You're just too damn close."

She stepped back and he released her, chuckling deep in his chest. "Sorry, Detective, didn't mean to make you..." His pause was thick with innuendo, "...whatever I made you."

Sam stared at him, searching for an appropriate response. Finding none that wouldn't just prolong the agony, she spun around hastily, half stumbling as she made her way back to the car. Even though she could no longer see him, she felt his gaze, burning into her, hotter than the inferno of the fiery sun.

****

Sam's mind was barely on her driving as she headed back to the station. The man was exasperating; unlike anyone she'd ever met. Oh, she'd met his *type*. Married one, in fact. But she'd never known anyone who could so thoroughly befuddle her thinking, throw her off her game like he could. She would have to be very careful around Doctor Dexter Hawkins. Keep contact to a minimum. A *professional* minimum.

She glanced in her rear view mirror, noticing a car behind her that she thought she'd seen at the ball field. It was a late model silver Nissan Maxima. She couldn't see the driver very well, but a chill washed through her that told her she was being tailed.

As if her noticing him prompted him into action, the car drew closer. Seconds later, she heard the impact and felt her car lurch as the Nissan bumped her from behind. Gasping, she tightened her hands on the wheel and glanced in the rear view mirror. She couldn't get a good look at the driver, other than to tell that he or she wore sunglasses and a ski cap. She couldn't even say for sure if it were a man or a woman.

She picked up her cell and increased her speed, but before she could dial, she felt a thump and heard the grinding of metal on metal. The phone flew from her hand and she skidded out of control, her car leaving the roadway in a heart-pounding instant. She slammed on the brakes, but it was too late. She was heading straight for a light pole. The car jolted violently and she was thrown forward, then back against the seat. The airbag didn't deploy, which probably meant the impact wasn't hard enough, although it certainly felt like it was.

It all happened so fast, she wasn't sure whether or not she'd been injured, figured if she had been, she'd feel the pain soon. Dazedly, she peered out the car window, hoping to get a closer look at the driver, even though she was sure the car was long gone.

She was surprised to see the vehicle moving slowly, nearly at a crawl, just ahead of where she'd crashed. Unable to reach a pen and paper, or her cell, she quickly made a mental note of the plate number just before the car sped away.

Disengaging herself from the seatbelt, she groped around the front seat and floorboard, searching for her phone. Now the pain had started, a sharp, stabbing from her shoulders up through her head. She felt a sudden wave of nausea and managed to scramble from the car before she vomited.

Stumbling around to the passenger side, she opened the door and spotted her cell phone in the floorboard, far under the glove compartment. She grabbed it, relieved to see it was still on, therefore working, and dialed the station.

As she waited for assistance, she took long, deep breaths, hoping she could keep from fainting. She was sure it hadn't been long, but it seemed like eons passed before an ambulance arrived.

A young female EMT hopped out of the driver's side and rushed over to Sam. Another EMT opened the back doors and slid out a gurney.

"Here, let us take a look," the woman said, lowering Sam to the gurney. "Are you okay?"

Sam shook her head, then nodded. Or maybe it was the other way around. "I'm fine," she slurred.

She heard tires screech and saw Frank climbing out of his Crown Victoria. He rushed to her side the moment he spotted her.

"What the hell happened, Spike?"

Sam shook her head and lifted a hand to wipe the hair back from her face. Her fingers came back wet and sticky. She stared down at the red dampness, not quite understanding.

"Ah, Jesus." Frank turned to the female EMT. "Can you help her, please?"

"Yes, sir, we're taking care of her. Don't worry."

The young woman poured some liquid onto a gauze pad and began carefully dabbing at Sam's forehead. It hurt like a son of a bitch, but she tried not to let on.

"So, what happened?" Frank studied her worriedly.

Sam explained everything, even gave him the plate number, if she remembered it correctly.

"Soon as they're finished with me, we'll go check it out," she told him.

"*We*, hell. You're going to the hospital."

Sam shook her head, causing the EMT to admonish her to stop moving. "I'm fine. I'm going with you. Get on it while it's still fresh. Could have something to do with the..." Suddenly, the word she was searching for left her. It was right there, then, *poof*, it vanished, as if it were some foreign word she couldn't quite remember.

She looked helplessly up at Frank and he nodded, as if pleased she was suffering head trauma just so he could be correct. "That's what I thought. You're going to the hospital and I'll follow up on this. See if it has anything to do with the *investigation*."

Damn. That was the word.

Chapter Six

The hospital kept Sam overnight for observation but determined it was only a mild concussion and released her the following morning. When Frank arrived to take her home, he looked her over thoroughly. "How ya doin'?" he asked.

"Better now that I'm out of there. How bad is the Impala?"

"Not too bad. It's in the shop, but there's a rental waiting for you at your place."

"Great. Thanks."

As soon as Frank dropped her off, she called the station. The captain ordered her to take the next few days off and she argued vehemently. "I'm in the beginning of a case. I can't just stop now. You know the first forty-eight hours—"

"Have already passed," he interrupted. "Stay home, get some rest, come back Friday. Not one day sooner, you got me?"

Friday. This was Wednesday. So, all of today, all of Thursday, she'd be sitting around here, going stir crazy. *Shit.*

"Fine," she agreed, only because she knew it wasn't a request.

She swallowed two of the pain pills the doctor

had given her and crawled into bed, thinking maybe she'd sleep for two days, then it would be time to go back to work.

****

She wasn't sure how long she'd been out when the alarm clock went off. What the hell? Why would she set an alarm when she wasn't going into work? Then she realized. Wasn't the alarm clock. The damn phone.

"Hello," she mumbled into the receiver.

"Samantha?"

She scowled, trying to clear the fuzz from her brain. The voice sounded familiar...

She sat straight up, jerking the blanket to her chest with one hand, clenching the phone with the other.

"Dex?" she said, belatedly realizing she'd used his first name.

"Yes. You okay?"

"I'm fine, I was just..." She didn't know whether to say 'napping' or 'sleeping' because she had no idea what time it was. The pills had knocked her out. She peered at the digital numbers of the clock on the nightstand. Five o'clock in the evening.

The room was dark because the heavy drapes were pulled. Was it...? Must be Thursday? She'd slept for twenty-four hours. Good Lord. She thought she wanted to sleep until time to go back to work, but she hadn't really meant it. "I was just napping."

"Oh. Sorry I woke you."

"No, I needed to wake up anyway."

"You're not working?"

She didn't want to tell him about the accident. "No. I'm off today. What's up?"

"I have the hair analysis results."

"Already?"

"Yeah. Fast work, huh?"

"Yes, thank you. Was she a user?"

"If you want to come over, I can give you the

results."

She furrowed her brow. "Can't you tell me over the phone?"

"I could, but you're really going to want to see this."

She sighed. Yes, she did want to see it and with all the sleep she'd gotten, she was probably more than fit to drive to his office. "How long will you be at the morgue tonight?"

There was a pause. "I won't. I meant come over to my house."

Sam's heart stilled. His house? "I don't know..."

"Up to you. I suppose I can run them over to you tomorrow, if you're going in to work?"

"I am, but I don't want to wait until then. Ok. I'll come over. Give me your address."

****

The man stood at his kitchen sink, looking out the window to his front yard. All was quiet, peaceful this morning in his neighborhood. He liked that. Enjoyed the calm. Especially after what he'd been up to lately.

He lifted the glass of water to his lips and drank, noting his hands no longer shook, at least not as much.

Of course, this time he hadn't killed. He only ran the cop off the road. He never intended to hurt her. He just wanted to get her attention. And he was certain he had. Certain—clever detective that she was—she'd taken down the license number. All according to plan.

Something outside caught his attention and his breath nearly stopped. A police car, slowly moving down the street.

The shaking started again and he slapped the glass down on the counter, flinching at the thudding noise it made, the sound peculiarly loud in the silence of the house.

Reaching up, he yanked the curtains closed,

leaving a small gap to peer through.

Had they found out it was him in the car or were they here about the judge?

He gulped in a terrified breath when the cruiser pulled to a stop next to the curb in front of his house.

Both hands on the lip of the sink now, he gripped so tightly, he could feel the edge dig into his palms.

The car door didn't open, no one got out. The person inside, a man it looked like, seemed to be on the phone, although he couldn't see clearly from this distance.

His entire body trembled as he waited for whatever was to happen. Was the officer calling for backup? Was he verifying this was the address of the suspect?

He had a decision to make. Answer the door to the officer, act innocent, and hope like hell they had nothing on him, or make a run for it. But where would he go? He had no friends to help him hide out from the cops. Had no relatives to speak of, not any who would risk their asses for him.

No. He couldn't imagine being on the lam. Wasn't his style. He'd never survive. *You just have to stay and take your chances.* Even if it means going to prison. His eyes filled with tears at the thought. He'd never survive in prison. No way in hell. They'd eat him alive.

Preoccupied with his horrific woolgathering, he all but missed what was happening outside. A whoosh of relieved air left his body as the cruiser drove away.

He sent up a silent prayer of thanks while at the same time realizing this had been a warning. He had to be careful. Smart. He wasn't cut out for the business of killing. That much was glaringly apparent. But he had to suck it up and go on. There was more work to be done.

The small television in the kitchen was on, the

sound so low he almost missed the report, but he heard the words 'Judge Mona show' and grabbed the remote, zipping up the volume.

An Asian woman, mic in hand, stood in front of Valiant studios. She was giving an update on the murder of Judge Mona Morrison, sadly informing the public the police had no suspects at this time.

He peered beyond the woman to the building that housed the Judge Mona staff.

A tingle of anticipation worked its way through his body.

"Don't go far," he whispered to the reporter. "You'll be back there sooner than you know."

****

Downtown traffic was heavy but once Sam merged onto I-75, it thinned out considerably. Good thing. She was starting to feel a little woozy. A wave of nausea swam through her chest, lodging at the base of her throat.

She clamped a hand over her mouth and pulled over, rolled down the window, and sucked in long breaths of the fresh air, being careful to breathe through her mouth. She hadn't eaten anything in the past twenty four hours. She should have grabbed a bite before heading out.

After a few minutes, she was feeling marginally better, but still a little lightheaded. She considered going back home, but decided that since she was closer to Hawkins' house than hers, she would continue on to his.

Whatever he had for her, it had better be good.

Hawkins lived in a neighborhood in the suburbs and she followed his directions to a brick house with pale yellow siding. A silver GMC truck sat in the driveway. She was surprised to see that he owned a vehicle other than his precious Harley. The space next to the truck was empty, so she assumed the pampered Harley was parked in the garage.

The flowerbed outside the front window held no

living flowers or plants, unless you counted weeds. She rang the bell and almost immediately, Hawkins opened the door. He wore a blue chambray shirt with a dish towel slung over one shoulder. And, dammit, he was wearing those faded Levis.

He invited her in and led her into a living room. Sam smelled something cooking, Italian, she guessed, and her stomach rumbled.

"Sorry about the lack of furnishings," he apologized.

'Lack of furnishings' was a gross understatement. The walls were completely bare, except for stacks of cardboard boxes resting against them. Two black leather recliners with consoles containing cup holders and remote caddy's faced an HD big screen television. A Reds' game was on, the sound muted.

"Wow," Sam said, admiring the size and clarity of the picture. "Adam Dunn isn't nearly that tall on my TV."

Dex laughed. "Yeah, it's pretty cool. You like baseball?"

"Love it. My dad used to take me to games when I was a kid."

"Being from Boston, I've always been a Red Sox fan, but I'll have to admit, I like the Reds."

Sam smiled. "I was born during the seventh game of the '75 World Series. My mom was furious because Dad didn't make it to the hospital until the game was over."

Dex shrugged. "Can't blame him. That was one hell of a series."

"Yeah," she said, turning to face him. "And we kicked your ass."

"I wouldn't exactly say you—" He stopped, his gaze shifting to her forehead. Frowning, he gently brushed her bangs aside. It was the merest whisper of a touch, but it caused a shiver to run through her. "What happened?"

She pulled away. "I just had a little accident."

"Accident? What kind?"

"A car accident. It was a few days ago. I'm fine."

"Here, sit down, can I get you something to drink? Aspirin?"

"No, really, I'm fine." But she did sink into the soft leather recliner. She was once again feeling a little lightheaded.

He stood looking down at her. "I'm such an ass," he said, shaking his head.

"What?"

He sighed heavily. "We could have done this over the phone. All I wanted to tell you was that the test was negative. There were no drugs in her system."

"Then why did you have me come over?"

"I wanted to see you." He shrugged. "I wanted to cook dinner for you and I didn't think you'd come if I invited you."

Unbelievable. She opened her mouth to blast him, but closed it again. The dinner smelled great. And she was starving. "What'd you cook?"

He smiled. "Lasagna."

She returned the smile. "Smells wonderful."

A few minutes later, they were seated at an oblong dining table, Caesar salads, lasagna, and crusty French bread laid out before them. Not caring if it were ladylike, Sam dug into the food, finishing half before she spoke.

"This is fantastic," Sam said when she finally took a break. "A man who can cook. Wow."

"Actually, this is the only thing I know how to cook." He grinned sheepishly. "I had an Italian girlfriend a while back. She taught me how to make it. To her, food was erotic so she shared her passion. The relationship didn't last long enough to learn how to cook anything other than lasagna."

"Ah," she smiled. "I feel better now. I was afraid you were going to show me up. But, I can cook two or three dishes, so I still have you beat."

"If you can cook two or three dishes, how is it that some man hasn't already snagged you up?" he asked teasingly.

"Actually, I was snagged up, then tossed back."

"You're divorced?" At her nod, he said, "What kind of idiot would divorce you?"

She flushed, unaccustomed to compliments from men, especially one as devastatingly handsome as Dex. "I guess I'm just not very lovable." She'd meant to come off flip, but it hadn't worked. She said hastily, "I didn't mean to sound self-pitying. I'm happy with my life as it is. Getting married was the worst mistake I've ever made."

He reached across the table and covered her hand with his. "No. Marrying the wrong person was the worst mistake you've ever made."

She gave a nervous laugh and pulled her hand away. "Yeah, well, I figured out a long time ago that I'm not good at picking the right person. Best just to stay alone." She'd meant to say 'single', but had said 'alone'. God, was she sounding pitiful or what?

Fortunately, he changed the subject. "Ready for dessert?" The question was innocuous enough, but somehow, coming from his lips, it sounded sexual. Their eyes met and she saw that he knew what she was thinking. His lips turned up at the corners in a slow smile. "I have pound cake. From the bakery."

It took her a moment to answer. "I couldn't eat another bite. But thank you." Her voice sounded breathless and she was suddenly nervous. She needed to get the hell out of here. She stood and began clearing plates.

"No." He reached out and closed his hand over her arm. "Don't bother with this. I'll get it."

Her gaze went down to where his touch warmed her flesh, making little tingles shoot clear to her toes. She took a deep breath and pulled away from him. "I insist. You did the cooking."

"You're not feeling well and you're my guest."

"Ok," she acquiesced. "Thanks. I really should be going anyway."

"You know, I'd feel better if you'd let me give you a ride. I was a jerk to trick you like that. The least I can do is drive you home."

She narrowed her eyes. "What was that all about, by the way?"

"It was a pathetic attempt to spend some time with you, get to know you better."

"Why?"

"Because, I like you."

"Like me? How can that be? I've been nothing but rude to you since the day we met. You can't possibly *like* me."

He shrugged and held out his hands, palms up. "You got me there. Okay. I am very, very attracted to you. I admire you and I respect you. I think that under that hands-off, tough-gal exterior, there's a passionate, sensitive woman."

"I guess that proves my point. You don't know me at all."

He stepped closer and Sam held her breath but didn't retreat.

"I'd like to. One thing I do know." His voice was soft, seductive, drawing her in. "If you'd try this..." he reached up and took hold of her jacket, slipping it off her shoulders, "...and this..." he pulled the banana clip from her hair, letting it fall loose around her face, "...you'd look soft, feminine, beautiful." His husky tones and glittering eyes made her shiver in response.

She reached up and self-consciously smoothed the crease she knew her hair must have. It was still damp when she'd pulled it back. "As opposed to?" she asked, a catch in her voice giving away the effect he had on her.

"As opposed to strong, intimidating, beautiful."

"Hawkins, I..."

His eyebrows lifted in amusement. "If we were in bed together, would you still call me Hawkins?"

"I guess we'll never know, will we?" she said, but the words came out in a shaky whisper.

He took a strand of her hair where it rested on her shoulder and caressed it between his thumb and forefinger. "Never say never."

Oh God, this was insane. He was a real piece of work.

Be strong, Samantha, you know his type.

Then she remembered poor Anthony Conniver, his wife...Dex. What an idiot she was. She'd almost fallen for his charm.

She jerked away from him, grabbed her blazer and shrugged it on.

"Hey, what's wrong?" Dex asked

She whirled back to face him, her voice rising as she spoke, "*You're* what's wrong. Good Lord, do you think I don't recognize a player when I see one? You're one of those men who thinks because you're sexy, you can treat women however you'd like, screw with their emotions."

She knew she was being unreasonable, bitchy even. But she'd had her heart trampled by guys just like him. The first had been when she was sixteen. By the time she miscarried his child, he was already dating her best friend. She'd been stupid enough to marry the second one. Yep, she knew the type. So, thanks, but no thanks.

"I don't know why you'd be interested in me, anyway," she said scathingly. "After all, I'm not wearing a wedding ring."

He scowled, his voice rising to match hers. "What's that supposed to mean?"

She started to tell him, then decided against it. He knew exactly what she meant and she wouldn't play into his innocent act. "Nothing. Never mind."

"It's not 'nothing'. What the hell are you talking about?"

Before she could answer, there was a sound at the doorway of the kitchen and Samantha turned to find a young boy and a woman standing behind her.

"I'm so sorry," the woman said. She was attractive, though slightly overweight, and blonde with wide, cornflower blue eyes. The boy was about fifteen or sixteen, tall, and also blonde. He would no doubt be a looker when he'd aged a few years.

Sam remembered seeing him at the ball field. Dex's son? And, this woman must be his wife. Or, please God, his ex-wife, since Sam was alone in his home with him.

"Ryan forgot his cell phone and we came back to get it," the woman continued. "If I'd known you had company, I'd have knocked. I didn't mean to interrupt." She flashed an apologetic smile at Sam.

Okay, must be his *ex*-wife.

"Oh no," Sam said quickly. "We're colleagues and had business to discuss. You're not interrupting anything."

"It's fine," Dex agreed. "Detective Colby was just leaving." The cold tone of his voice hurt a little, although Sam had no idea why. Hadn't she just read him the riot act?

"I'm Clarissa and this is Ryan." The woman stuck out her hand and Sam took it.

"Nice to meet you both," Sam said, then turned to Dex. "Thank you, Dr. Hawkins. Goodnight."

Their eyes locked for one quick moment before Sam quickly made her exit.

Chapter Seven

Sam was glad to be back at work, although she felt the lingering effects of her collision in every muscle, not to mention the pounding headache that wouldn't go away. Her car was out of the shop, seemingly no worse for the accident.

While she'd been gone, Frank had run a check on the license plate of the car that hit her. Her hopes soared when they learned the car belonged to none other than Calvin Rollins. They dipped back down again when she found out that Rollins had reported the car stolen, *before* Sam had been run off the road.

If the killer was trying to frame Rollins, it made sense he'd use the guy's car to go after Sam. And that could explain why he'd hung around long enough for her to get the license plate. He wanted them to know the vehicle belonged to Rollins.

The car was found abandoned late last night and the lab was running prints, but Sam didn't hold out much hope they'd find any that belonged to the thief.

In her absence, Frank had also checked out the alibis of the other Judge Mona litigants on Sam's list. Everyone came back clean. That left Todd Brahern, Eric Avery, and Calvin Rollins on the prime list of suspects.

As Sam was leaving the station that evening, a woman approached her outside the precinct doors. Sam didn't recognize her at first. The evening sun was behind her, casting her features in shadows. Then Sam saw who she was and her stomach clenched. What was Dexter Hawkins' ex-wife doing here?

Clarissa smiled as she approached. "Oh, good. I'm glad I caught you."

"What can I help you with? I was just leaving."

"Can we go grab a coffee? I wanted to talk to you."

Sam hesitated, looking for a gracious way to decline the invitation. None immediately came to her, so she accepted, dread and curiosity winding through her in equal measures.

They walked down the street to the *Java Joint*, standing in line long enough for Sam to wonder when 'grabbing a coffee' had begun to mean sipping five dollar concoctions with names like 'Mocha Madness' and 'White Line Flavor' from a paper cup and tipping for counter service.

When it was finally her turn, Sam chose a Columbia blend—sans the exotic flavors—and joined Clarissa Hawkins at one of the high tables with shiny wooden tops.

Sam took a cautious sip of the hot brew, looking at the woman expectantly.

"I'm here about Dex," she said. "I wanted you to know what kind of man he is."

Sam frowned. "Why do I need to know what kind of man he is?"

The too-blue eyes regarded Sam shrewdly, making her feel as if she were strapped to a lie-detector. "I sensed there was something happening between you two." Clarissa shrugged. "I could be wrong, but I don't think so. I just want to make sure you don't hurt him."

Sam laughed and shook her head. "*Hurt* him? We're business colleagues, nothing more."

"Ryan is not Dex's son," Clarissa said, not disputing or acknowledging Sam's assertion. "He's his stepson, but you couldn't tell it by the way Dex treats him. As a matter of fact, Ryan lives with Dex instead of me because Dex is the better parent. I can't say I'm proud of that, but it's the truth. Dex moved here from Boston for Ryan's sake. Ryan was having some trouble at his old school and Dex felt a new environment might be better for him. So, he uprooted his own life and moved, for Ryan. He even coaches Ryan's baseball team. They're a group of kids who've been in trouble and Dex is trying to get them interested in something besides raising hell."

And Sam had accused Dex of taking a day off to play when he'd actually been helping troubled teens. *Nice.*

She had to admit she was grudgingly impressed at Dex's sacrifice, but she still wondered what it had to do with her.

"Sounds like an amazing man," Sam said, half facetiously. "It's a wonder you let him go."

Clarissa gave a small, sad smile. "Biggest mistake I ever made. I'll never find another man like him."

"Right. Perfect men don't come along every day."

She grinned. "He's not perfect. He has his faults. Such as, he is definitely not a morning person. Don't even talk to him until he's had his first cup of coffee. He's a monster."

She said it affectionately, almost reverently. As if she were saying, 'he rescued orphans from a burning building and was awarded the Nobel peace prize.'

"Sometimes he has horrible nightmares. He used to be in this Black Ops organization and his nightmares can get pretty intense. One night, he grabbed my neck and the look in his eyes..." She shuddered. "But, he woke up right away and was very apologetic." She flushed. "And he most definitely made it up to me."

Sam suddenly realized she didn't like the image of Clarissa and Hawkins in bed together. What the hell was wrong with her? He was nothing to her. Why should she care? Sam gave her wristwatch a quick glance like she had somewhere to be.

Clarissa didn't seem to notice. She obviously wasn't finished with the Saint Dexter Hawkins Tribute. "He's also *way* too into sports. Drove me crazy that he had to catch every football and baseball game he possibly could." She laughed. "He wanted to plan our honeymoon around a Packers game. Wanted me to go to Green Bay, Wisconsin for my freakin honeymoon! Can you believe it?" Her gaze turned pensive. "I put my foot down. Refused. You know what?"

Sam shook her head, not sure if she wanted to know 'what'.

"I should have let him." She smiled wistfully. "If I had it to do over again, I'd have gone to Wisconsin, or even the Antarctica, for my honeymoon, anywhere, just to be with him." Clarissa wiped at the corners of her eyes. "Sorry, didn't mean to get all sappy on you."

"Sounds like you still love him."

"Oh, yes, I do. And if you have feelings for him, if you have even a smidgen of interest in him, you hold on and don't ever let go."

"Why are you telling me this if you love him?"

"Because, I lost my chance with him and I want him to be happy."

"Surely it's not too late for you?"

"Yes. I'm afraid it is. I had an affair. Dexter is fiercely loyal and expects the same from those he loves. He has forgiven me, but he would never give me another chance. I killed his love."

Fiercely loyal? Must not extend to wives of other

men. "I'm sorry."

She shook her head. "Don't be. I'm lucky to have him in my life."

"I'm still not sure why you came to see me. Why you're telling me all this."

"Because he cares about you."

"We barely know each other."

"Maybe. But I saw the way he looked at you. Trust me, I know him. Don't screw it up."

Before Sam could respond, her phone rang. It was Mona Morrison's station manager.

"I understand you wanted to speak with me?" Carson Clayton said.

"Yes," Sam replied, casting a look at Clarissa. "Would now be a good time?"

"Any time. I'm at the office now, will be until much later in the evening. Have a lot of catching up to do since I took those few days off. You know, you wanna play, you gotta pay."

"I know the feeling. If it's okay, I'll be there in, say, half an hour?"

"Sounds good. See you then."

Sam stood and held a hand out to Clarissa. "Thanks for coming to see me. I'll keep what you said in mind."

The woman held her grip for several seconds, meeting Sam's eyes. Finally, she released her, nodding and saying softly, "Please do. For your own sake, please do."

****

Sam drove to the television station as dusk fell, bringing even cooler temperatures, although there had already been a break in the oppressive heat.

A light summer rain fell, the wipers languorously slapping away the moisture from the windshield.

Sam put in an Elvis CD and cracked the window just a bit. She loved the fresh smell of rain in the air and didn't figure a little moisture would hurt anything.

Love Coming Down, one of Elvis' more obscure releases from the 70's, was playing and the damp evening air and Elvis' powerful voice filled the car, surrounding her, calming her. She released a breath and along with it, some of the tension of the past few weeks.

Sometimes, she felt as though she were being tugged on from too many different directions and there wasn't enough of her to go around. She was afraid that one day, she'd be wrenched into a thousand pieces and just disappear.

There was her job, her family with their problems, their holidays, their never-ending functions. There was her mother with her guilt trips about Sam's absence from said functions, her criticism regarding Sam's lack of family devotion, not to mention Sam's ring less finger and barren womb, circumstances that were specifically aimed to punish *her*. And now, there was Hawkins' ex-wife with her perplexing praise of a man who'd divorced her. And Hawkins himself, with those incredible eyes and devastating dimples and his paradoxical good boy/bad boy persona.

But mostly, there was Mona Morrison, the victim who cried out from the grave for justice.

Sam lowered the volume on the CD player when she arrived at the guard shack. After checking her badge and confirming Clayton was expecting her, the security guard waved her through.

She parked where he directed and eased the window closed. She climbed out of the car, not bothering with an umbrella, even though the rain was falling a little harder than it had been.

The building was dark, abandoned, looking completely different than it had when she'd visited less than a week ago. The hum of activity and swarm of people were absent, lending it a deserted feel. Sam shivered, feeling creeped out, which made no sense. After all, she was armed.

She passed the sound room where she'd watched the tapes with Giselle, then the recording studio, warily checking to her right and left as she did so. She could hear the rain hitting the roof. The sound she'd enjoyed only moments before now gave off an ominous vibe.

At the end of the hallway was Clayton's office. Sam knocked but there was no response. She pushed the door open and stepped inside. The room was dark, except for the glow of a fish aquarium standing against one wall next to a bookshelf. Colorful fish glided through the water, darting in and out of a small castle resting on the bottom.

"Mr. Clayton?" Sam called.

No answer. She caught a shadowed figure in her peripheral vision and whirled, her hand flying beneath her jacket to her shoulder holster.

An embarrassed laugh left her throat when she saw what had startled her. It was a life-sized cardboard cutout of Judge Mona Morrison. It stood just inside the door to the left, hidden from her view until she'd stepped inside.

Sam shook her head and glanced around the room. Something still didn't feel quite right. Clayton was supposed to be here working all evening. Even the guard had thought he was here. He could have gone to the restroom, or maybe a break room for a cup of coffee. But the entire building felt deserted. As if she was the only living human here.

A clattering noise broke the silence, like something shaking around inside a box. It sounded like it was coming from this room, but she couldn't identify its source.

She pulled her weapon and glanced behind her. Nothing.

"Mr. Clayton?" she called again, moving further into the room.

She made her way cautiously to his desk and

when she peered behind it, she saw him. Or, at least, she assumed it was him, even though she'd never met him. He looked to be in his mid- thirties, short, neat brown hair and a goatee. Nice-looking man. Well, he had been a nice-looking man. Now he was a corpse.

He was lying half in, half out of his chair, his eyes wide and staring, his mouth contorted in a death grimace. His flesh was reddish and swollen, one eyelid slightly drooping.

Sam holstered her weapon and grabbed her lapel mic, calling for an ambulance as she knelt to check him. Putting her fingers against his pulse, she confirmed he was beyond help.

Despite the physical characteristics she'd noticed on his face, she didn't see any visible signs of injury. Did he have a heart attack? He wasn't old, but even the young were susceptible to heart problems. Sighing, she stood. As she did, she noticed a mark on Clayton's neck.

Two small holes. Fang marks.

Sam went numb and at that moment, the clattering sound resumed. Only this time, she recognized it. It was a rattle... A snake.

Once more, she drew her weapon. She stood stock still, unable to look for the snake, afraid she'd find it.

She was terrified like never before in her life, even more so than the time a coked-out thug with a pistol had her cornered. She'd taken a bullet then, but she'd trade that time for this one in a heartbeat, no doubt about it.

Yes, she was armed, but this was a *snake*. A quick, deadly, *hidden*, snake. One that had killed once and undoubtedly wouldn't hesitate to do it again.

She shuddered, her gun hand quaking. If she could get a shot at the snake, she'd blow it away and to hell with PETA. But that was the problem, she couldn't see it. The demon serpent was slithering around somewhere in the dark.

Her breathing was quick and shallow, loud. She couldn't control it, even though she feared it would alert the snake to her presence. Sweat broke out at her hairline and trickled down her face, underneath the collar of her jacket.

What was it she'd heard on one of those Discovery channel programs? That if you were perfectly still, a snake wouldn't attack? Or was that a bear?

Snake or bear...snake or bear...snake or...

Fuck it! She ran.

Chapter Eight

Sam was still trembling as the animal control officer held the snake in a large white bag after lifting it with a pair of long tongs and slipping it inside.

"This is a Mojave Rattler," the man said. He was young, short, and thin, with dark hair that fell over his forehead, causing him to make a constant slinging motion to get it out of his eyes. His voice rose in pitch and he spoke with rapid excitement. "It's one of the most dangerous snakes in the US. Their venom is like, ten times more toxic than any other rattler." He shook his head. "These puppies live in the Mojave desert out in California, maybe some in Texas. Don't know how it got here."

Don't know either, but get it the hell away from me. Sam wanted to scream the words at him but she nodded. "Thanks. We'll check into that."

"Pretty good bet the killings are about the show now, huh?" Frank said after the happy snake boy had gone. He peered closely at Sam. "You okay, Spike?"

"Yeah," Sam laughed. "Just discovered I have a fear of snakes. Didn't know that."

"Hell's bells, who *doesn't* have a fear of snakes?"

"That guy, apparently," Sam replied, jerking a thumb at the retreating animal control officer.

"Got to be the same doer, even though the MO is different." Frank worried the drinking straw clenched between his teeth. "Isn't Avery from Texas?"

"Not *from* Texas, but he moved there. You're thinking because the rattlers are found in Texas, it might be a link to him?"

"Might be."

One of the uniforms approached. "Detective, Ms. Corinthia is here. She's in the lounge down the hall."

Sam nodded and she and Frank went to the lounge.

Giselle Corinthia stood in the center of the room, her face taut, stress clearly showing in the eyes and in the lines around her lips. She wore a shiny gold, floor-length, body-hugging dress, proving what Sam had suspected when she met her the first time. The woman was perfect.

Sam could almost hear Frank salivating as he stood behind her.

"Ms. Corinthia," Sam said, extending a hand. "This is my partner, Frank Torino."

"Pleased to meet you," Giselle said. Frank nodded like a bobblehead but didn't respond as he shook the woman's hand. His face was a study in reluctance when he released her.

"I was at a banquet when I received the call about Carson. Is he...dead?"

Sam nodded. "I'm afraid so. Would you please take a seat? We need to ask you a few questions."

Giselle nodded and moved gracefully to the sofa, floating downward until she was perched on the edge. Sam sat next to her and Frank took the chair positioned caddy cornered to them.

"Do you know of anyone else working late this evening, other than Mr. Clayton?" Sam asked.

Giselle shook her head. "It wasn't common for

anyone to be here after hours. The cleaning crew comes in at night, but normally, the staff leaves by six or so. Carson was only here because he had a lot of catching up to do after being out of town."

"Tell us about the cleaning crew," Frank interjected. "You guys have your own staff or you use a service?"

"A service. I have the name and number if you'd like." She closed her eyes and said. "How was he killed? Was it the same way as Mona?"

Sam glanced at Frank. "We're not at liberty to discuss details at this time. We're investigating the possibility it is the same killer, but we can't know for sure just yet."

Giselle opened her eyes and nodded. "I understand."

"Would you know of anyone who works here who has a special interest or knowledge of exotic animals?"

"Exotic animals?" Giselle echoed. "You mean, like tigers?"

"No, more like..." Sam almost couldn't say it, but she cleared her throat and continued, "...reptiles. Snakes."

Giselle's eyes widened. "Snakes? You mean like, serpents, like real, live *snakes*?"

"Yes."

"Oh my God, is that how he..." Her face paled and her fingers nervously pleated the silky gold material resting on her thigh. "Oh God," she repeated.

"Miss Corinthia, could you please answer the question?"

"Well, no, I have no idea about that. I've never heard anyone mention anything like that."

"Anyone make a trip to California lately that you know of?"

Giselle sighed, shook her head. "No, I'm sorry. I wish I could be more help."

"You're doing fine," Frank said. "Just relax. Can I get you a water or something?"

"No. Thanks. I'm good." She smiled wanly. "It's a little freaky, you know? I mean, what's happening around here?" She gave a delicate shudder. "Makes me want to rethink my career choice. You know, now it looks like the killer would have to be someone from one of the shows. Except..." Her brows drew together and she shook her head, quickly, briefly. "No. That's crazy."

"What is it? Nothing is too far-fetched. We need to hear anything that might be related."

"Oh, it's nothing, really. Just that I kind of wondered about Vin. He and Mona were always fighting, he always wanted to take and take from her. Then, he'd go off partying, fooling around with all these beautiful young women. Making Mona feel like dog shit, you know?"

"But did Mr. Rollins know Mr. Clayton? Would he have any reason to want to hurt him?"

One shoulder lifted in a shrug. "I just thought, maybe. You know, since Mona and Carson were sleeping together."

****

"Did you know about that?" Frank asked, speaking to Sam, but watching Giselle's hips sway as she left.

"The affair or that you have the hots for Ms. Corinthia?" Sam teased.

"The affair," Frank replied, his face coloring.

"No. Had no idea. Could figure into the murders, though. I mean, if the boyfriend killed Morrison and knew about the affair, makes sense he might go after Clayton."

"We'll check his alibi. Go have a chat with him."

"Yeah, but the problem with the alibi is we have no idea when the snake was planted."

"True. Still won't hurt to talk to the guy."

Walburn appeared in the doorway of the lounge.

"ME's here," he told them.

"Thanks," Sam said, her heart pounding almost as fast as it had over the snake, although she refused to analyze the reason.

On trembling legs, Sam reluctantly made her way to Clayton's office. Even though she knew the snake was gone, it didn't keep her from being a tad nervous. After all, it was possible they ran in packs, like wolves or something.

Dex was squatting next to Clayton's chair, his gloved hands turning the corpse's face in different angles. He looked up when Sam and Frank entered and gave Sam a quick smile.

"Hey there, Doc," Frank said. "Whaddaya think?"

"Cause of death looks like a snake bite."

"Yep, thought so."

Dex straightened. "I'll let you know my findings as soon as I do the prelim. Unless you want to attend again?"

Sam shook her head. "No, thanks. One autopsy a week is enough for me."

Dex nodded. "Okay, then. I'll try to get to it tomorrow. Probably the same killer. I want to do whatever I can to help stop him before he kills again."

"Thanks, our feelings exactly," Sam replied.

The three of them walked outside, standing together in the still-falling mist, and watched as the body was loaded into the coroner's van.

When the van drove away, Dex cast a quick glance at Frank, then at Sam. "Can I talk to you for a sec? In private?"

Frank lifted his brows, giving Sam a curious look. "Sure." He nodded. "I'll call in and see if we can get a location on Rollins. Maybe we can talk to him tonight."

"Great," Sam replied, wondering what Dex could possibly want. "I'll just be a minute."

After Frank left, Sam and Dex stepped beneath the awning, out of the rain. Dex studied her for a moment, sighed, and shoved his hands in the pockets of his jeans. "I heard you found the body. Found the snake."

"Yes." Sam shuddered involuntarily. "What about it?"

"I just...I want you to be careful. I mean, this guy is dangerous and I don't want anything to happen to you."

A warm flush spread through her and for a moment, she couldn't speak. She wasn't accustomed to men worrying about her. "I'll be fine. Despite what Hollywood leads moviegoers to believe, killers seldom go after the cops on the case. Plays well on screen, but it's not reality."

"Maybe. But come on, the car accident, the snake. Who knows what might happen next?" He removed his hands from his pockets and reached out to take one of hers. "I care about you. I just want you to be safe."

Don't care about me, please don't care about me because I could find you way, way too hard to resist and I don't need this. Not again.

Sam tugged her hand from his and forced a professional note to her voice. "I appreciate your concern, Doctor Hawkins, but I can assure you, the department is taking every precaution to keep the officers on the case safe."

She met his eyes and thought she saw a brief flash of hurt, but he only nodded and said, "That's good to know, Detective. I'll contact you with the autopsy results."

Sam thanked him and hurried away, not looking back as she climbed into the shelter of her car.

****

The killer brought the frosty mug of beer to his lips and took a long, grateful swallow. All around him, voices rose in conversations ranging from the

69

unusual heat wave, to the presidential election, to the Reds' chances of making the playoffs.

Normally, he'd join in, but now his attention was riveted on the television behind the bar. Once again, just as he'd predicted, the news crew was on location at Valiant Studios. This time, the reporter was a man, tall, thin, wearing a raincoat and squinting in the drizzling rain. The sound was muted but words scrolled across the bottom of the screen in white on black captioning.

Reports have not been confirmed, however, sources say a man was found dead this evening in an office at Valiant Studios, where the Judge Mona show is filmed. The identity of the victim has not been released, but it is rumored that authorities suspect foul play.

As you may recall, a week ago today, on the morning of July 11th, Judge Mona Morrison was found dead in her home. Police are investigating the possibility that these murders are connected.

Stay tuned to WYKG news, we'll update you as more information becomes available.

He tightened his grip on the mug. A shiver ran through him that was part fear, part elation. *It worked.* He couldn't believe it, but it had actually worked. The snake had fucking *killed* the guy.

He took another swig of the beer, his attention so captured by the news report that the voices around him merged into one resounding, indistinguishable jangle.

This just in, the transcript on the screen continued, *early reports, although not confirmed, indicate the victim is station manager, Carson Clayton.*

He just barely refrained from pumping a fist in the air.

Yes!

For a brief moment, he'd been concerned. It had occurred to him that his slithery friend may have targeted the wrong victim. After all, snakes were probably indiscriminate killers. But now he was certain. Clayton had been the recipient of the rattler's toxic venom.

Inside, he was filled with a strange mix of glee and terror. Quite possibly, he was smarter than the cops. He was actually getting by with murder.

It's all for a good cause, he assured himself. They deserved it, each and every one of them. And he was ready for the next phase. *Willing* and ready. The willing part was what really freaked him out. When had he morphed from reluctant slayer to joyful executioner?

He allowed himself a small grin behind the beer mug as he marveled at how easy this murder thing was becoming.

Chapter Nine

Frank told Sam that when he called Calvin Rollins' apartment, his roommate said that Vin was out, most likely at his favorite nightclub, *Bonger's*, which was the place he'd invited Sam to.

Frank and Sam rode together to the club. The parking lot was packed, but they parked next to the sidewalk near the door—one perk of being in law enforcement.

As soon as she exited the car, Sam could hear music booming from the club. It was loud, some kind of new age rock and roll she didn't recognize and most definitely didn't enjoy. Who knew that, at thirty-three, she could be so out of touch with what was hip in the music industry?

Her 'out of touch' vibe increased when they went inside and most of the patrons looked half her age. That, combined with her blazer, slacks, and unflattering ponytail, made her feel old and frumpy...and she didn't give a damn. She'd take old and frumpy over this obnoxiously loud, claustrophobia-inducing bar any time.

She and Frank made their way through the bodies, some laughing and drinking, some dancing to the beat of the music, even though they weren't on the dance floor. Sam's headache was coming back. She'd almost rather slam her noggin into the car again than continue listening to the excruciatingly loud pounding of the music that literally shook the ground beneath her feet.

Looking around the crowd, she spotted Rollins over by the bar, chatting up a girl with piercings and spiky, multi-colored hair. Sam tapped Frank on the shoulder and pointed, saving her voice for when she'd have to shout at Rollins to be heard over the club noise.

Rollins looked up as they approached and the 'I'm all that' smile disappeared from his face when he recognized them.

"Can we have a word with you?" Sam yelled.

His eyes darted to the girl, then around the bar, and back to Sam. He shrugged as if to say 'Do I have a choice?'

Sam took him by the arm and led him over to the bathrooms where the noise level was at 'unbearable' as opposed to 'deafening.'

"Do you know Carson Clayton?" Sam asked.

Rollins' handsome face scrunched into a scowl as if the effort of thinking was foreign to him. "Mona's station manager?"

Sam nodded. Frank stood behind her with his notebook, ready to jot down any words of wisdom the genius might spew.

"No," Rollins said. "I mean, I know who he is, but I never met him. Why?"

"He was found dead this evening." No reaction. "Did you know he and Mona were sleeping together?"

His face tightened and he shook his head. "I don't believe that."

"Because, why would she, since she had a stud like you?"

His full lips stretched into a smug smile. "Something like that."

73

"Well, that's the talk around the water cooler. We figured if you knew, it might give you a reason to dislike the guy."

Rollins shrugged. "It's a free country. We weren't married. And it's not like I didn't have other bitches, you know?"

Sam let that one pass. "You know anything about snakes?"

He gave her a puzzled look. "Like, what about them? Like, they're scary as shit? I know that much."

"You ever own any?"

"Fuck, no. Whassup with this shit? I'm trying to hang out and chill and you're givin me grief."

"Sorry if a murder investigation is cramping your style," Sam shouted, her voice growing hoarse from having to yell above the racket. "That's all we have for now, but I would advise you to be available in case more questions come up."

"Am I a suspect?" His face suddenly looked pale, even with the fake-bake thing he had going on.

"Let's just say you're a person of interest. We'll be in touch."

She and Frank threaded their way back through the crowd, which seemed to have increased in numbers, if that were possible.

Finally, they were out in the cool, fresh air and Sam took a deep lungful of it before turning to Frank.

"What do you think?"

"Huh?" He cupped a hand behind his ear. "I think my eardrum's busted." He shook his head. "Damn kids."

"What do you think about Rollins? Does he look good for it?"

Frank shrugged. "Don't know. He seems like a punk, but a killer? Not sure I get that vibe from him."

Sam didn't either, but so far, she hadn't gotten

74

that 'vibe' from anyone. And she needed to. Before the killer claimed another victim.

****

Sam arrived at the chief's house just as evening chased away the last remnants of the day's heat.

The home—correction—mansion was an enormous red brick and limestone structure with a wrap-around porch and french bay windows. Small, trickling fountains lined the walk, leading to an ornate mahogany door. The front room was gargantuan with a high, oak-beamed ceiling and a massive stone fireplace flanked by stately white columns.

The party was being held in a large ballroom off the living area. Elegant chandeliers sparkled above the party-goers, picking up the glinting highlights of jewels and finery of the women, offset by the men's stylish tuxedos.

The chief had not amassed his fortune with the salary the city paid him, generous as it was. He'd married money in the form of Eliza Wessel, an heiress whose family made their fortune building luxury resorts around the world.

Sam stepped inside the ballroom, suddenly feeling conspicuously alone as she gazed at those in attendance—so coupled up, she'd almost think they were passengers from Noah's ark.

She sought out someone, anyone, she might know, some small, ridiculous part of her hoping Dex would be here.

Her dress was a satin, ruby-red strapless, slit high on one thigh, making her feel self-conscious and daring at the same time. She felt, if not beautiful, at least pretty.

She didn't want to talk to Dex, didn't want to even see him, but—although she'd never considered herself vain, she wanted *him* to see *her*. Wanted him to see that she could be an attractive woman. She refused to scrutinize why she gave a damn what

75

Dexter Hawkins thought of her.

Frank approached, looking almost presentable in a black tux jacket over an ocean-print shirt. He was accompanied by a tall, red-haired woman wearing too much make-up and revealing too much cleavage.

"Hey there, you're a freakin' knockout, Spike. Who'da thought it?"

"Gee, thanks, Frank."

"This here's Shannon."

Sam and the woman exchanged greetings and the three made small talk for a few minutes before Shannon tugged on Frank's arm and led him out to the dance floor, leaving Sam alone again.

Sam glanced around, looking for the bar, and spotted Dex standing across the room on the other side of the dance floor. She only caught glimpses of him as the dancers parted. She turned away, not wanting to be caught staring. After a few moments, unable to resist, she let her gaze wander to where she'd seen him, but he'd disappeared, and she tried to tamp down her disappointment.

"You look amazing."

Sam nearly gasped at the sound of Dex's husky voice so near. She turned to face him, a little shiver running through her, the breath catching in her throat.

"Thank you. So do you."

And he did. He wore a charcoal gray tuxedo with a satin lapel, a white wingtip shirt, and silver vest. His hair had been trimmed but the dark blonde edges still brushed the collar of the tux jacket.

The corners of his mouth lifted in a lazy, dimpled grin. "Can I get you a drink?"

"Yes, please. A vodka tonic."

"I'll be right back."

Before he could walk away, she reached out to stop him. He glanced at her hand on his sleeve, then his gaze lifted questioningly to hers. "You need something else?"

She released her hold and said, "I wanted to ask you about Clayton's autopsy."

"Oh yeah, sorry. Meant to give you a call when I finished up this evening. The autopsy showed cause of death was the snake bite and he appeared to have been dead for a very short time."

She nodded. "That makes sense. I spoke to him just a few hours before I arrived."

His gaze slid down her body, then back up to her face, his eyes meeting hers, seeming to convey an unspoken promise. "Just for tonight, how about we eighty-six the shop talk? You look too beautiful to be discussing corpses."

She couldn't speak. His nearness and his devastating smile caused her throat to close up and her heart to beat faster than it should, so she simply nodded.

"I'll be right back with that drink." He bestowed another flash of dimples upon her before weaving his way through the crowd.

Sam watched as he stood waiting for their drinks, noticing that someone to his right had caught his attention. When Samantha followed his gaze, she saw Rachel Conniver. Her husband, Anthony, stood by her side. As Sam watched, Dex made his way toward the couple and Sam's insides clenched. Surely he wasn't going to make a scene, right here in front of everyone?

Although, that quickly, he'd shattered her affable mood, and once more pissed her off, she didn't want a big blow-up at the mayor's birthday party.

Thinking she may be able to defuse a bad situation, she worked her way to the bar and approached the threesome just in time to hear Anthony Conniver say, "What the hell is your problem?"

"No problem, buddy, just wanted to say hello to

Rachel."

"You mean my *wife*?"

Apparently, Anthony had heard the rumors.

Dex's face blanched and his gaze went to the woman. "Your wife?"

Dex hadn't noticed Sam yet, but she spoke behind him. "Dexter, I was looking for you. I think you owe me a dance."

He whirled, looking at her without speaking, and for a second, she thought he was going to refuse, thought he'd rather stay and fight over this woman than dance with her. But after a slight hesitation, he said, "Yes, that's right."

He took Sam's hand and led her onto the dance floor. She got a whiff of his cologne, a light, masculine scent she didn't detect until he pulled her close against his body. Too close. The contact immediately sent ripples tingling along her flesh, adding to her conflicted state of mind.

"What the hell were you doing, flaunting your affair right here, in front of her husband?" she said in a low hiss.

"Affair? For one, we're not having an *affair*. We went out a couple of times, that's it. For two, I damned sure didn't know she was married."

"Right. That's what they all say."

"It's the truth. I would never, ever do that. Especially after..." He trailed off, shook his head. "Never mind."

Especially after his wife cheated on him. She knew that, but he probably didn't know she knew. And she wasn't going to let him off that easily. Some devil inside her made her keep pushing. She didn't like herself much for it, but that didn't stop her.

"No sense pretending," she said, letting her voice drip with sarcasm. "Guys like you need the challenge, the rush, the sense of living on the edge. Don't try to fight it, just let the beast run free."

He gazed at her incredulously and shook his

head. "You *want* me to be the villain, the bad guy, don't you?"

She shrugged. "You just make it easy."

She felt him tense, then a heavy sigh left him and he released her. He stared down at her, not touching her. Eyes that had, just moments ago, held a hint of desire, were now filled with disgust. Without a word, he stalked off the dance floor.

Sam stood there, deserted in a sea of couples, stunned and embarrassed.

And knew she deserved it.

She'd been wrong to taunt him like that. It was immature and spiteful. They were professionals. They had to work together. She owed him an apology.

Through the archway of the ballroom, she saw him leave out the front door and she followed.

She stepped outside and looked out over the lawn, for a moment thinking she'd lost him. That he'd disappeared that quickly. But then she spotted him heading out toward the gardens on the south side of the property. She made her way down the porch steps as quickly as she could, which wasn't as quick as she'd like, thanks to the six-inch heels she was unaccustomed to wearing.

She caught up to him in a little clearing in the center of the garden and for a moment, she was so astounded by the beauty of the setting, she nearly forgot her purpose for being there.

A wall of brilliant hibiscus, orchids, and various plants surrounded a koi pond, the water so clear, the colorful fish were like vibrant little beacons beneath the surface. A trickle of water fed over rocks into the pond, the sound soothing and mesmerizing. The garden was lit only by the meager light coming from the pond and the shine of the moon peeking through the fronds of the plants. Two small iron benches sat on either side of the pond and a stone wall secluded the courtyard from the rest of the property.

Sam was shocked that other party guests hadn't ventured out to this little piece of paradise. She and Dex were its only inhabitants.

He stood with his back to her, hands in his pockets, as immobile as the stone wall he faced. He must have heard Sam approach because he whirled to face her, his eyes narrowing with recognition.

"What do you want?"

"Just to talk."

His body seemed tense, as if he were holding himself in check. He was silent for so long, she thought he was going to simply ignore her until she went away.

The only sound that broke the stillness of the evening was the trickling of the fountains and the light breeze dancing through the leaves of the foliage.

When he finally spoke, his voice was hoarse, as if the words were forced out of him. "No talking." He moved slowly toward her, stalking like a jungle cat. "If you stay out here, I'll do exactly what I've wanted to do since I met you."

"I just came to...I need to apologize," she stammered.

"This is your last warning. My restraint won't hold out much longer." He closed the remaining space between them and looked down at her.

The moonlight reflected in his eyes, giving them a jewel-like hue, an otherworldly glitter, as if a mythical creature had inhabited his body and taken human form for some unknown purpose. Perhaps it was to sustain this constant, churning unease she felt every time she was around him.

"Run away, Samantha Colby," Dex said softly. "If you know what's good for you, you'll leave while you can."

Chapter Ten

She didn't run away. She stayed right where she was, looking up at him, feeling her heart nearly jumping out of her chest. She swallowed and her lips parted, but she had no idea what she was going to say.

It didn't matter, because before the words could form, he growled and tugged his hands out of his pockets, reaching out and crushing her to him, making her gasp for breath.

He brushed his lips across hers, then planted kisses along her jaw line. She shook her head in weak protest, at the same time dropping it back to allow him better access to her throat. He obliged, abrading the tender flesh with his whiskers, a sensation that was slightly painful, yet highly erotic at the same time.

She made a half-hearted sound of protest and he gave a low chuckle.

"You can't deny what's happening here, Samantha." Her name dripped like honey off his tongue. His words were nearly as seductive as his touch and she wanted him—with equal fervor—to both shut up and keep talking.

"I don't...I can't..."

Alicia Dean

"You can," he murmured hotly against her neck.

Yes, her mind screamed, but this was a mistake, a big one.

He brushed a hand across her collarbone and her nipples tightened. His knuckles skimmed along the sensitive peaks and she sucked in a breath, warm moisture pooling between her thighs. Every square inch of her flesh was tingling hot, alive, yearning and aching with need. It had been so long since a man had wanted her. So long since she'd wanted a man. And never had she wanted one like this.

She strained her upper body toward him and he took her breast in his hand, kneading it through the satin material while his thumb moved in slow circles around the tip. His other hand cupped her bottom, pressing her against the tightness in his slacks.

"Okay, okay, okay," she panted, grabbing his face between her hands, her fingers touching the rough stubble along his jaw. She ground her lips against his, her tongue delving inside, tasting the essence of mint and brandy and man.

"Yeah?" he asked huskily between kisses.

"Oh yeah," she groaned. "I can't do this anymore. I need you."

"Yes," he whispered triumphantly, brushing his lips along her bare shoulder and working kisses downward, to the vee between her breasts, then, *oh God, yes.* His hot, wet mouth latched onto a nipple and she gasped.

"Please, make love to me," she begged huskily, groping at his shirt, pushing it back off his shoulders.

His mouth left her breast and he stared down into her eyes. "You sure?"

"I'm sure," she said breathlessly.

He reached behind her, found the zipper and tugged until it came loose. The silk slid down her body, pooling at her feet. She wore nothing but a strapless red bra, thigh-high hose, and garter belt. The night air caressed her bare skin and she shivered. She felt wanton and sexy and oh so turned on.

"God, you're beautiful." He bent his head and kissed the tops of her breasts. Her skin tingled, tightened with wanting him. She placed her hands on the back of his head, feeling his silky hair beneath her fingertips. Pressing him more tightly to her, she thrust against his seeking mouth, urging him on.

"Please, now, I need you," she moaned. "Let's do this thing and get it out of our system."

She felt a subtle change in him that her passion-glazed mind couldn't comprehend. He went motionless. His head lifted and he looked down at her, holding his fully clothed body against her nearly naked one. The desire in his eyes was gone, replaced by... What? Disappointment? Anger?

"This *thing*?" he bit out.

She nodded slowly, confused, her body still craving satisfaction.

"How long has it been?" he demanded in that same clipped tone.

"What? How long has what been?"

"Since you've been with a man. Since you've had sex."

"What does that have to do with—"

"Because, it appears you may have agreed simply because you need a fuck."

She flinched at the harshness in his expression, in his tone. But he was right. She hadn't had sex in a very long time. So, yes, she probably did need it.

What he didn't understand, and what she was only now coming to realize, was that she didn't want sex with just any man. That's why she hadn't had it in so long. She wanted it with this man. But that was foolish. Foolish and dangerous. She couldn't afford to lose her heart to a man like him.

"Sure," she said, forcing nonchalance into her tone. "Isn't that what you need?"

He stared at her, his eyes going hard as flint. His lips curled into a humorless smile. "I did, yes. Suddenly, though, the urge is gone."

And she knew—because their bodies were still pressed together—that he was telling the truth. His erection had disappeared.

Nice job, Samantha, you managed to un-*turn on a man.*

She felt tears at the back of her throat as her desire, although more slowly than his, ebbed away.

He pulled back and goose bumps shivered over her flesh. She snatched the dress up, hurt and humiliated, fumbling to step into it while he stood and watched, arms crossed, a look of contempt on his face. He didn't offer to help and finally, she managed to get dressed.

His gaze latched on to hers for just a moment, then he shook his head and stalked out of the courtyard, his footsteps echoing along the stone path.

Sam sank onto one of the wrought iron benches and sat in the near dark, amidst the trickling fountains, traces of passion still lingering, feeling bereft and inexplicably, very, very sad.

****

The party ruined, and knowing the chief wouldn't notice her absence, Sam headed home. At least she'd made an appearance.

She stuck the key in the lock but froze when she realized that the door was already unlocked. She knew, knew without a doubt, she'd locked her door. She was a cop living in a big city. She *always* locked her door.

Heart hammering in her chest, she tried to work out how to proceed. She didn't have her weapon. It wouldn't fit in her evening bag and she figured she wouldn't need it at the chief's party. She had her cell phone, but she'd feel like an idiot if she called Frank, or 911, and no one was in her apartment.

She kept a gun in the drawer of the table next to the front door. If someone was in her apartment, she could most likely get to it before they got to her.

Taking a deep breath, she twisted the knob and cautiously pushed the door open.

Her television was on, as was her kitchen light. Moving quickly, she stepped inside and yanked the drawer open, retrieving the gun and whirling just as a man came out of the kitchen.

He stared at her in surprise, then a big grin split his face. An intruder, but not a stranger. She'd rather it had been a robber than the man standing in her apartment.

"Hey, hey, baby, no need for firearms."

Yes, there was an *immense* need for firearms. She hesitated, put the .38 back in the drawer and slammed it shut, then turned to face her ex-husband.

Chapter Eleven

"What in the hell are you doing here and how did you get into my apartment?"

"I came because I wanted to see you. I was able to get in because I still have a key. You didn't change the locks. Must mean you *wanted* me to get in."

"You're out of your fucking mind, Shane. Get the hell out, now."

"Come on, don't be that way." His eyes swept over her body. "You look gorgeous, by the way. Hot date? If so, I guess it didn't go so well. You came home alone."

His words stung more than she'd have thought. Yes, she'd come home alone. Because she'd screwed up with Dex. Which was good, she told herself firmly. Things were best left on a professional level. And the asshole standing in front of her most definitely confirmed that she didn't need a man in her life.

She studied him, noting the difference three years had made. He looked a little older, but was still attractive in a Satan's minion sort of way. His hair was longer, the dark showing a few strands of gray. She was surprised that, with the size of his ego, he wasn't coloring it. Probably wouldn't be long before he did. His hazel eyes were the same, although there were more lines around them now.

"Tell me what you want and leave," Sam demanded. "Did you run out of my money? I'm surprised it took you this long."

"It was *our* money," he corrected, and she let it pass, not reminding him that *she* was the one who'd earned it all. "But, I was wrong to take it all. I should have left you your half." He smiled as if he'd just bestowed a great favor on her. She glared at him but didn't speak. "Anyway, I came back because I wanted to see you."

"Well, now you've seen me and I'm just as boring as I always was. So get the hell out of my apartment."

He sighed and moved further into the living room. Plopping down on the couch, he said, "I don't have anywhere to go. Tanya kicked me out. I'm between jobs and I thought I could count on you. I mean, we go back a ways and I know you won't turn me out." He looked up and gave her that charming smile that once made her melt. Now, it only annoyed her.

"You have a lot of nerve," Sam said through clenched teeth, pacing in agitation. "I haven't heard from you since you walked out on me and you think you can come back because you're destitute? I don't give a damn about you, your breakup, or your sad state of finances. I want you out, now."

He stood, surprising her with the hint of tears in his eyes. "I know I did you wrong and I don't blame you for hating me," he said quietly, making his way to the door. "I'll leave you alone."

Sam didn't hate him. She felt nothing for him. How had she ever been stupid enough to feel anything for this shallow, self-centered man? She'd been comparing Dex to him from day one, but Dex was nothing like him.

Shane would never have been worried that she

might be harmed by a killer on a case she was working, as long as her paychecks kept coming in. Shane would never have been concerned about her being injured in a car accident. And he would never, ever have put his own sexual needs aside because he thought she didn't care about him enough. He would have taken what he wanted, gotten his satisfaction, and not given a damn if she 'felt' anything for him.

She let out a long sigh and shook her head. "Wait."

Shane stopped at the door and turned around, his eyes alight with hope. "Yeah?"

"I'll give you some money to help you get back on your feet, but you have to promise you won't ever bother me again. Not ever. Do you understand?"

His face fell. "You don't even want to try again? We once had something really special."

"Sex is not 'special,' Shane. Love is. And we never had that. Do you want the money or not?"

He nodded vigorously. "Sure, yeah. I really appreciate it."

She went to her desk and took out her checkbook, writing him a check for five-hundred dollars. She didn't owe it to him. He'd damn sure taken enough from her already. But she wanted to be rid of him and if nothing else, she was grateful to him for making her see that she hadn't lost anything when she'd lost him. For making her see that not everyone was as they appeared. Dex was a good man. And she'd blown it.

She ripped out the check and handed it to him. He looked at the amount and she saw him wage an inner battle.

Surely, he wasn't going to demand more? If he did, she'd take the check back and show him the business end of her .38. She could only be pushed so far.

Maybe he saw something in her eyes when he raised his head, because he nodded and opened the door.

"I mean it, Shane," she said, allowing a note of menace to enter her voice. "I better not see you around here again. You got it?"

He nodded. "Sure, yeah. And thanks, Sam. I was a fucking idiot to let you go."

"Yes, you were," she said, closing the door firmly behind him.

Chapter Twelve

Sam was at her desk Monday morning, poring over the case notes, when Krista Turpin called.

"I'm not sure if it's any help, but I thought you should know. I found out there was a note."

"Any idea what it said?" Sam asked.

"No, but Keith's sister told me he'd for sure left a note and that Todd still has it."

Todd had claimed there was no note. And he actually had it in his possession?

"Thanks," Sam said hastily, ending the call. She grabbed her keys and headed out the door to find Mr. Brahern.

Brahern wasn't in, but his friendly, pregnant receptionist told Sam she could wait in his office. Sam paced the small room, glancing out through the glass walls for Brahern's arrival.

As she waited, she studied his office, searching for anything that might raise a red flag. Nothing visible, but it wouldn't hurt to do a little in-depth exploration. Might as well make use of whatever time she had.

She went around to his side of the desk. His computer showed a screensaver from the television show 'House.' A nudge of the mouse and the screensaver disappeared. Sam opened his documents file, not sure what she expected to find. As she searched, she kept looking out the glass, making sure no one noticed what she was doing. They all seemed busy with their own tasks and as far as she could tell, weren't paying attention to her.

Each document she came across appeared to be work related—insurance forms, claims, letters to customers.

Frustrated and most likely running out of time, she gave up and started for the opposite side of the desk. As she did, her gaze fell on something sticking out from underneath the large desk calendar. It was just the corner of a paper, but it caught her attention because it was blue and older looking than the other paperwork. Sam pinched the edge and pulled it out. Written on blue legal pad paper was the suicide note.

To my family,

I'm so sorry, but I can't do this anymore. I've felt like a failure all my life and after the whole world saw what that bitch did to me, everyone will know that is exactly what I am. A failure.

When she called me a whiny little mama's boy, I could once again hear Dad's voice, screaming in his drunken rage, "Whiny little mama's boy!" Then the snap of the leather as he cut me with the belt. I can actually feel the pain of his huge fists slamming into my face.

Todd, I know he treated you the same, but you were always the strong one. I'm sorry most of all to you, because you are the only person in this world who truly loves me, truly understands me. I didn't realize, not until she reminded me, that all I will ever be is a failure, a whiny little mama's boy.

That phrase won't leave me. It pounds into my brain day and night. But I know how to make it go away.

Please forgive me,

Your brother, Keith

The paper was stained with dark reddish brown spots. Blood. Sam's fingers shook as she realized what she held in her hands. Motive.

"I was afraid it would come to this."

Sam drew in a sharp breath and looked up. Todd Brahern stood in the doorway. In spite of the heat, like Sam, he wore a jacket. She could see a cylindrical object outlined in the pocket. A gun.

"Hello." Sam smiled, trying to slip the note back where she found it. "I hope you don't mind. Your receptionist said I could wait in your office." But why would she be behind his desk? She didn't have an answer for that one.

He shook his head. "No need to pretend. I know you saw it. I know you've figured it out. Of course, after Krista's death, I might have been caught, anyway."

Sam's heart pounded loudly and quickly in her chest. "You killed Krista?" Sam had just spoken to her, so it would have had to be recently. Was that where he'd been?

"Not yet. She was next. *Will* be next, after I figure out what to do with you. It's already set into motion. I just hadn't counted on this little complication." His lower lip trembled and his eyes filled with tears. The pocket holding the gun began to shake. His voice was high and quivery as he said, "But a cop. Shit, shit, shit. Did *not* plan on killing a cop."

Sam's insides squeezed. She would rather face a cold, calculating killer than an excitable, unstable, novice who wasn't accustomed to handling a firearm. Too many variables there.

"Look," she said evenly, "just take it easy and we can work this out."

His eyes darted from side to side, his head shaking regretfully. "Too late for that." He motioned with the hand inside the pocket. "Come on. Me and you are going for a little ride."

Sam tried to remain calm and think the situation through. It was doubtful he'd shoot her here with all the witnesses. If she went with him, he'd be a lot more likely to kill her.

"No way." She shook her head. "Not going anywhere."

"You realize I have a gun?"

"Yes. But I also realize you won't shoot a police officer with so many witnesses."

His face scrunched and more tears rolled down his cheeks. His head swung briefly toward the glass window, then back to Sam.

"You're right." The hand swiveled until it was pointing toward the outer office. The pregnant receptionist stood a few feet outside the window at a copy machine. She saw them looking at her and lifted a hand in a cheery wave. "But I'll kill her. Sure, there are witnesses and I'll go to jail. But how will you live the rest of your life with her blood on your hands, Detective?"

Shit. She'd underestimated him. She wasn't sure if he'd do it or not, but she damn sure couldn't take the chance.

"That's what I thought." He must have seen the surrender on her face. "Nice and easy, slip your weapon into that top right drawer."

One of the first things she'd been taught at the academy was to never give up her weapon. But, there was no way she could let an innocent woman die to hold onto it.

Sam did as he instructed and he nodded. "Very good. We're going to get along just fine."

He swiped at his tears, then stepped to the side of the door and motioned for Sam to precede him. When she didn't move right away, he raised his eyebrows and stared at her questioningly.

Gritting her teeth, shooting him a menacing glare, she stalked ahead of him out of the building.

The sun was warm, midway in the sky. A light breeze blew through Sam's hair. A beautiful morning. Too beautiful a day to die.

Sam walked slowly in front of Brahern, hearing his rapid breathing behind her. She hoped his finger wasn't actually on the trigger. The man was way too edgy to be in full control of his muscles.

In the insurance agency's parking lot, Sam saw Dex, sitting on his Harley a few spaces away from her car.

Shock momentarily froze her as he climbed off the bike and approached, stopping in front of her, staring uncertainly into her eyes.

"What the...? What are you doing here?" she managed to say beyond the tightness in her throat.

Brahern had halted directly behind her. She could feel the tip of the gun barrel in her lower back.

"I stopped by the station to talk to you and I saw you pulling out of the parking lot. I followed you."

"Why?" Her mind searched frantically for a way to use this unexpected distraction to overpower Brahern, but nothing occurred to her that wouldn't endanger Hawkins and the innocent citizens milling about.

"I wanted to..." he glanced over her shoulder at Brahern, then his gaze went back to Sam. "Can we talk alone?"

"Hi," Brahren said. "Detective Colby is taking me to the station for a statement. I think I may have some information in the Judge Mona case, so we're sort of in a hurry."

"Yes, I'm sorry. Now is really not a good time," Sam said, studying the details of Dex's face, committing them to memory, just in case it was the last time she saw him.

"It will only take a second. I wanted to apologize for, you know..."

A warm trickle slowly worked its way through her. He looked shy, embarrassed, and utterly irresistible. Suddenly, she wanted to cry, but instead, she smiled. "No need to apologize. But we'll talk later, okay?" Sam tried to keep the catch out of her voice but wasn't successful.

Dex frowned, glanced at Todd once more, then nodded. "Sure. I'll call you."

Hawkins climbed on his Harley and slid the helmet over his head. He waved as Brahern halted Sam next to the Impala. He instructed her to open the door and climb in on the driver's side, then slid into the passenger seat next to her. When they left the parking lot, Hawkins was still sitting on his bike, watching them drive away.

****

Sam drove slowly, following Brahern's directions, mentally reassuring herself that everything would be okay. She'd figure a way out of this.

Brahern was no match for her skill, although his hysteria, not to mention the .22, might give him a slight edge. In the passenger seat next to her, the man was a wreck.

"Oh God, this is getting out of control," he muttered. He tapped his forehead with the heel of his hand. "Think, think, think. There has to be a way... No, I have to, I have to kill a cop."

"You don't have to," Sam said calmly. "It's not too late to stop this. We can get you help."

He shook his head vigorously. "I killed two people."

"You killed Mona Morrison and Carson Clayton." It was a statement, not a question. He'd just confessed, but it wouldn't do her any good if she didn't live to tell someone. At his nod, she asked, "How'd you get the snake in Clayton's office?"

"I didn't. I hired a guy to handle it all for me." He barked a short, nervous laugh. "It's the damndest thing. Did you know you can get pretty much anything on the black market these days? Not just

95

drugs and guns, but all kinds of stuff. Even deadly snakes and someone to plant them for you."

Yes, she knew that, but how did an insurance salesman from the Midwest know that? "Who planted it for you?"

"Oh, no. I'm not giving you names. In case you live, I'll be as good as dead if I squeal. I paid a guy ten thousand dollars—took it out of my retirement plan—and he handled everything. Got the snake, bribed someone in the cleaning crew to let him take their place, planted the snake, yada yada yada."

What he didn't know was, if she survived, he'd just given her a place to work backward from, starting with the cleaning crew. Key word 'if.'

"Why are you doing all this? Because of your brother's suicide?"

They were now on the highway heading east. She passed a cruiser, wishing she could signal to him, but with the .22 gyrating around in the car, she wasn't going to take a chance.

"Keith was my baby brother. I protected him all his life. Until he..."

A sob tore from his throat and he covered his mouth with his non-gun hand. He closed his eyes tightly, briefly, then swallowed and went on, "That bitch humiliated him. Our father made our life hell growing up, then Keith married Krista, and she broke his heart. Just when he was getting his life back together, she takes him to court and humiliates him in front of millions of people. So, I killed the judge with her own weapon. The gavel she used to destroy people's lives. So, you see, it was poetic justice. Clayton aired the show in spite of me begging him not to. Clayton was a snake in the grass—a snake took his life. Poetic justice."

He took a deep breath and said quietly, "I promised my brother I'd take care of him. I didn't do everything I should have to save him, but I'm hoping what I do now will bring him peace."

Brahern instructed her to take the exit that led to the mall where Krista Turpin worked. It was a few hours before the mall opened and the lot was empty. He directed her to a parking space on the east side, away from the highway.

Still holding her at gunpoint, he ordered her out of the car. They walked for a few minutes until she finally realized he was leading her to the opposite side of the mall.

"Why didn't we just park on this side?" Sam asked.

"Don't want your car to be out in plain sight. The roads back there aren't nearly as busy."

He stopped her in front of a door barely noticeable in the bricks of the mall. The knob opened under his hand and Sam wondered why it was unlocked—wondered how he'd made all this happen—and how, if she was as good a cop as she'd thought, she didn't see behind his pleasant, unassuming exterior to the monster underneath.

The door led to blackness. Even though it was nine a.m and the sun was out, the darkened interior of the space made it seem like midnight.

"Move," he commanded.

Sam hesitated, knowing if she entered the room, her chances of getting help decreased dramatically.

"Look," he said, his voice rising in pitch. "I'm kind of starting to lose it here. I'm getting scared and I want this over with. You gotta do what I say. Now. Get in!" The last ended on a wheedling screech and when Sam still didn't move, he began to scream, "Get in, get in, get in...," quaking like someone having a seizure.

"Okay," she said, placating. "Just calm down and—"

But before she could finish, there was a deafening boom. Sam recognized it as a gun blast just before a sudden force struck her thigh, as if she'd been punched.

Then, she was tumbling backwards, slamming painfully against concrete, dimly aware she was falling down a flight of steps into the blackened pit. There was no pain in her thigh yet, but there would be. The splatters of blood landing on her face as she fell told her she'd been shot.

Sam wasn't sure which pain was worse, her head slamming against the unyielding concrete, or the gunshot wound that was now beginning to throb like a son of a bitch. Before she could decide, she hit bottom, and blackness took her.

Chapter Thirteen

Samantha's eyes flew open when a hot, piercing pain streaked through her leg and up into her chest. She clenched her teeth and bit back a moan, not wanting to alert Brahern that she was awake.

She was still in that all consuming darkness, unsure of how long she'd been out. Something cool and solid was against her back. Was she lying on concrete?

She tried to move, to come to a sitting position, but it only made the pain worse. Sweat popped out on her forehead and nausea swam up to her throat. She thought she might vomit, or maybe lose consciousness again. Taking deep, slow breaths through clenched lips, she willed the nausea away, forcing her mind to think this through, figure a way out.

The leg was bad. She'd taken a bullet and she'd lost a lot of blood. And the pain. Oh God. The pain. It felt as though someone had taken a hand saw and attempted to dismember her from the hip down.

She'd been shot before, in the shoulder, but that time she'd been taken to the hospital before the shock had worn off. Now she knew exactly what being shot felt like. And it hurt like hell.

A bright light flicked on—a flashlight—aimed at her eyes. She squinted, trying to see Brahern behind the glare.

"What are you doing?" she rasped, her throat raw, the nausea still clawing at her insides.

He knelt and placed the flashlight on the ground. The beam partially illuminated the murky space, but all Sam could see beyond Brahern were shadows of shapes. Boxes, maybe?

He gripped her shoulders, pulling her to a sitting position. She cried out as agonizing shards of pain ripped through the wound, burning a path through her entire body. When she was propped against the wall, she realized her hands were tied in front. She took deep, gasping breaths, a rush of tears streaming down her face. She was humiliated at her show of weakness, but the pain was so severe, she couldn't control it.

"Here." He squatted next to her and shoved a needle in her vein, pressing the plunger on a syringe. "There's a little pain killer for you. I don't want you totally pain-free, but if you're bawling the whole time, you won't concentrate on what I'm saying. I've wrapped your leg to help slow the bleeding, but of course, the bullet's still in there."

She wondered how and why he'd come to be in possession of injectable pain medication, but she didn't question him and didn't respond. Instead, she leaned against the hard wall, clenching her teeth, waiting for the pain to ease. After a few minutes, it did. It was still there, but now it was a dull throb. Bearable.

He picked up the flashlight and stood, towering over her in the semi-darkness. His face was partially in shadows, giving him the macabre look of one of those late night horror movie characters.

"What are we doing here?" she gasped.

"I'm going to make you part of the plan I already had in motion. I'm going to burn this son of a bitch down, and you'll get the blame."

"That's insane. No one would possibly believe I did something like that."

"You wouldn't think so, would you? But, I've left a few clues to make sure they will. I had to hurry, you understand, your role in this was a recent development. But, I planted an article I had on me about remote explosives, starting fires, so on and so forth, in your car. I spilled some gasoline in your trunk. When I give my statement about the way you talked during our drive, the way you changed your mind at the last minute about taking me to the station for questioning, how you rambled on and on about doing something in a big way to further your career—"

"You can't be serious."

He nodded rapidly. "Oh, but I am. I've left evidence that should lead them to the conclusion that you intended to start a fire so you could rescue people from the mall, but it looks like you were overcome by smoke and didn't make it. Sadly, you and several others perished in the fire. If they don't quite buy it, no matter. At least you'll be dead and you're the only one who suspects I murdered the judge." He offered a ghastly smile that stretched his face into a gruesome facsimile of a human being. His nerves must have calmed because, although there was still tension in the set of his face, he seemed more confident than he had earlier.

"This will never work. You can't possibly—"

"Yes, yes I can," he interrupted. "At first, I was a little freaked when I caught you in my office. But then, true inspiration hit and I came up with a foolproof plan that wouldn't implicate me, yet, you will be dead, as will that bitch of an ex sister-in-law. You know, kill two birds with one stone. Of course, a lot of other birds have to die in the process. But, I don't know them and it's worth it to me. They're simply casualties in my quest to destroy one particular bird...the red-beaked, large-breasted whore bird." He gave a guffaw of laughter. "Pretty clever, wouldn't you say? I just made that up. And see, this is the final coup de gras. Krista burned my brother. Now, she'll burn." A smile stretched his lips. "Poetic justice."

"How do you think you'll pull this off without dying yourself?"

"Not to worry, Detective. I have a remote detonator that will spark those." He shone the flashlight on an enormous mound of wadded newspapers and kindling. A gasoline can sat nearby.

"Once I'm safely at my alibi location, I'll detonate the spark and alight the pile. You, being injured and tied up, will be unable to do anything about it."

His eyes glinted maniacally in the dancing shadows. She had to do something. Now.

He was standing directly in front of her. Could she kick him in the crotch with her good leg? She may not have a lot of strength, but one well-placed kick could...

Could what? Provoke him to grab the pistol and shoot her again? This time in the head? Forget it. Weak, tied up, injured. She didn't stand a chance against an able-bodied man with a gun.

"We are directly underneath the store where Krista works," Brahern continued. "So she, at least, will most definitely die, as will you, before the fire can possible be contained. The ropes will be burned away, so the investigators will never know you were bound. That's why I have your hands in front of you. It would look suspicious if your remains are found with the hands in back."

The scenario he painted made her stomach roil. Her thigh was starting to throb even more, the pain rearing its head once again. He had it all figured out. Whether or not they believed she'd set the fire on purpose, she, along with Krista and countless others, would die. A slow, painful, horrible death. Frustration and helplessness coursed through her and she felt tears at the back of her eyes. But, she wouldn't cry for this son of a bitch again. She'd at least die with some dignity.

She wasn't ready to give up quite yet. Her mind worked frantically, searching for a solution. He was truly insane, delusional. Maybe she could use that to her advantage.

"Listen," she said, trying to keep her voice steady, to sound convincing. "You gave me an idea. But we'll need to work together."

He frowned. "What are you talking about?"

She sucked in a deep breath, wiping sweat from her brow with her shoulder. "I'm up for a promotion, trying to make rank to sergeant. This could be perfect for both of us. We don't have to kill anyone else, though. Only Krista."

He grinned skeptically. "You'd be willing to kill Krista?"

She thought hard, trying to recall how this had played out in her head moments before. "Yeah. I don't like her anyway. Her and those fake boobs, blonde bimbo thinks she's better than everyone else. How about if I could fix it where only Krista dies? I'll make it look like I was trying to save her, but she dies and neither of us are implicated."

His glance moved down to the ground, as if he were considering her offer. He looked back up at her. "How would you do it?"

How *would* she do it? She didn't know, couldn't think this through. She was hurting too badly. Her mind wasn't working like it should. "I would start a fire and rush in to clear the building. As I herd people out, I would come up behind Krista and knock her unconscious. In the confusion, no one would notice. It would look like she was overcome by smoke and unnoticed in the rush of people fleeing."

He smiled and her hopes soared. Until she

realized it was a mocking smile.

"Good try, Detective. But I don't believe you. I don't believe you would do it, or that it would work if you did." He shook his head. "Sorry. We're going with my plan. You won't make sergeant after all. However, it makes my idea even more convincing. Your desperate act was to ensure the promotion. Thanks for the tip."

She groaned and let her head fall back against the wall. Son of a bitch. What now?

He slipped a hand in his pocket and when he pulled it out, he held an object that he waggled back and forth. Her cell phone.

"I'm taking this with me, so if you were thinking..." He shrugged. "Well, you know, forget it."

He put the cell in his pocket and lay the flashlight on the ground. Picking up the can of gasoline, he twisted the lid off and shook the liquid over the pile.

The pungent odor of the fuel wafted over her, so strong she could taste it in the back of her throat. Eyes watering, she coughed and spat, trying to rid her mouth of the taste.

He dropped the can and turned to her, his gaze almost sympathetic. "I really don't want to do this, I hope you understand. I have no choice. God be with you." He didn't look back as he hurried up the stairs and opened the door. She had a few seconds of precious sunlight before she was once more left in the dark with the meager beam of the flashlight.

****

Sam must have lost consciousness for a few seconds, because she suddenly jerked awake. Fear returned with a vengeance when she realized the day hadn't been a bad dream. Her entire body trembled with the horror of her situation. Not only was she going to die, but so would numerous others.

She had to do something. But what? Her leg was starting to burn like hell and she was growing weaker by the second. She looked toward the stairs that led to the door. If she could reach them, maybe...

Maybe what? The door would be locked, right? Even if she managed to drag her body up the stairs? She gritted her teeth and let out a hiss of breath. She had to try.

She squirmed around to her side, inching along the ground toward the basement steps. It was slow going, excruciatingly slow...and painful. The mall opened in an hour. So, she had an hour?

Then it hit her. No, not an hour. Most workers surely arrived at least half an hour, maybe forty-five minutes, before the mall opened. She had no time at all. She stopped, resting her head on the hard concrete, willing back the tears that wouldn't quite go away.

Think, Samantha, think.

Something rolled out of her pocket and landed on the ground in front of her. A cigarette. The one she planned to smoke when she solved the case.

Well, you solved the case.

She let out a laugh that wasn't quite sane and with it sucked in a mouthful of the gasoline infused air. The laughter turned into a sob and tears streamed down her face, partly from the fuel, partly from despair.

Dammit, dammit, dammit.

A sudden thought penetrated her panic.

The lighter.

She reached into her pocket with her bound hands and gripped the lighter.

If she could get to the kindling, she could start the fire now. Before there were people in the mall. Right now, there could possibly be a security guard, maybe two, but they would have an excellent chance of getting out alive, unlike a crowd of shoppers. Even though it was Monday, there would be a lot of people here. There always were. Not as many as on a weekend, but enough. If there were security guards inside, and if they died, it would be horrible, but not as bad as a whole crowd of people dying...innocent men, women, and children.

Of course, *she* would die. That was a given. With her injury and the wooziness from the pain medication, there was no way she could escape the fire.

But it was the only way.

She didn't want to die, even though she didn't have a lot to live for other than her family and her job.

Wasn't now, when facing the end of her life, the time she was supposed to think about regrets? She wasn't sure exactly what she regretted. Not having children? Spending all her time and energy on her career? One thing for sure, she regretted giving Shane the five-hundred bucks. What the hell was she thinking? She didn't owe him shit.

She thought of Hawkins and knew one more thing she regretted. Perhaps nothing would have come of it, but she wished she'd given him a chance. Wished she could know what it felt like to fully give in to the desire between them. It was more than just physical, though, at least on her part. She felt something for him she hadn't wanted to examine.

She examined it now. Was it love? Maybe. Or something close to it. Not that it mattered. She'd blown it—treated him like *he'd* been the one to screw her over. She knew Dex wasn't the same guy she'd thought at first. Wasn't like those other jerks she'd known. She'd typecast him in that role from the moment she saw him and hadn't let anything sway her.

She pushed those thoughts aside. She had other things to worry about now. Like her own imminent death. If she had her piece, she'd end it quickly, because she sure as *fuck* didn't want to die by burning to death.

"I'm sorry, God," she murmured a hasty apology. It probably wasn't a good idea to use the 'F' word just before you went to meet your Maker.

She wasn't absolutely sure she was going to heaven, anyway. She believed in God, always tried to do the right thing...well, mostly. But she certainly hadn't been a saint. All she could hope for was that this final sacrifice might earn her some celestial brownie points.

Gripping the lighter, tears streaming from her eyes, she began the slow, painful crawl to the kindling.

Each centimeter was agony. The pain was an enraged beast, ripping, tearing, shredding her with its razor sharp claws. But she had to, just a little more.

As she drew closer, the smell of gasoline grew stronger and the tears increased, blinding her.

She was within a hairsbreadth of her target—close enough that she was sure she could toss the lighter into the pile and start the fire—when she locked up, just froze.

She couldn't do it.

Hysteria welled inside her, strangling her as sure as the fumes of the gasoline.

Oh God, oh God, oh God.

Was that a prayer or had she taken his name in vain? She wasn't sure, she was so confused, hurting, terrified.

You're going to die, a voice inside her brain insisted, *and you're going to let a lot of innocent people die with you. Is that what you want? Is that the way you want to leave this world?*

No, it wasn't. A pervading calm overtook her. She felt surprisingly serene, accepting.

She struggled those last few inches.

Her thumb swiped the flint wheel.

She tossed the lighter onto the pile.

Alicia Dean

Chapter Fourteen

Todd eased the door open and looked around. The parking lot was empty. The detective's car was on the other side, away from the busy road the mall sat on. Now, he just had to make it to the little tavern where he'd spent many hours drinking.

That would be his alibi. When they questioned him, he'd inform them that she changed her mind about taking him to the station. He'd tell them she'd rambled on and on, saying she was going to do something big to get everyone's attention, then she'd offered to drop him off somewhere. He'd asked her to take him to the bar, because he needed a drink. *She was really freaking me out*, he'd say, *I was glad to get away from her.*

Ducking his head, he started toward the street, hoping it wouldn't take long to catch a cab to take him to the bar. He was so intent on rehearsing how the rest of this would all play out, that he didn't notice the motorcycle right away.

The first thing he became aware of was the rumbling sound. He looked up and saw the massive bike, with the man he and the detective had bumped into sitting astride. *Oh, shit.* This was not part of the plan.

The motorcycle bore down on him, stopping only inches from where he stood. With his hand in the pocket of his jacket, Todd let his fingers close around the butt of the gun.

"Where is she?" the man demanded. "I saw her car, so don't bother to lie to me."

He was a large man, well over six feet tall. Todd was squat, flabby, out of shape.

But the gun was an equalizer.

"I'm afraid I don't know what you're talking about."

"You know exactly what I'm talking about," the stranger roared. "Where the hell is Samantha?"

"I'm sorry," Todd said, pulling the gun from his pocket. "But I can't—"

He didn't see the man move, but he felt the impact. The man's booted foot stomped Todd's leg, right below the knee. A biting pain, like someone was wrenching his leg apart at the kneecap, clutched him.

Todd screamed. The gun fell from his numb fingers. Bloody bone extended through his pant leg as bile surged through him, moving like the agony that ripped at his body. And then he was falling, and he knew he was about to pass out, hoped he was, because the pain...

"Where is she?" the giant demanded again, looming over Todd where he lay writhing on the pavement.

Todd wanted to tell him, but pain and fear had cut off his air supply, rendering him unable to speak.

The giant lifted his head and looked toward the mall. He must have noticed what Todd only just now did. Smoke, coming from the basement entrance of the mall. The detective had figured out a way to start the fire early. He didn't know how, but she must be pretty damned resourceful. Not to mention brave...and stupid.

Todd didn't care how she'd done it, he was just

glad she had, because now the man was running toward the building, leaving Todd alone.

Soon, the police would come. And maybe they'd get to him before the giant returned.

****

The temperature was unbearable. Sam never would have thought she could feel such intense heat without actually being on fire. Which, she very well could be, because she smelled the unmistakable odor of burning hair.

She looked at the stairs through the increasingly thick haze. Tears streamed from her eyes and nose, but now she didn't think she was crying, she thought maybe it was from the smoke.

Her odds of making it to the stairs were not good. Her leg was hurting like hell, and she would most likely be overcome by smoke before she could reach them. The odds that she'd actually pull herself up the stairs if she did reach them were even less. The odds of the door being unlocked, if by some miracle she did make it that far, were pretty much zero.

In spite of her fatalistic prognosis, her survival instinct overrode her left-brained logic and she began to use her upper body to pull herself toward the exit.

She coughed, feeling like her throat and chest were clogged with ashes. In some part of her terror-numbed mind, she wondered how the hell she'd ever enjoyed smoking.

The heat seemed to reach out to her as she inched toward the stairs. She'd lost a lot of blood. She was growing weaker and her leg now throbbed with raging pain.

After a few seconds, she raised her head to check her progress and she began to cry. She had moved mere centimeters. Maybe she was even further away, although she knew that wasn't possible. A frightening, self-defeating realization came over her. She wasn't going to make it. No way in hell. She was going to burn to death.

The thought barely had time to take hold when there was a sudden brightening in the room. Not from behind her, where the fire still burned, reaching ever higher toward the insulation in the ceiling, but from above. From the top of the stairs. She sensed a burst of fresh air and looked up.

Dex stood in the open doorway. When he saw her, he rushed down the stairs. She had time to think of something she'd heard about how firemen...what was it? They rushed into buildings most people are rushing out of? Had that been from a movie? She couldn't remember and she didn't have time to think about it any more because Dex was there, lifting her in his strong arms.

She cried out as a sharp pain stabbed through her leg, but it was the best pain she'd ever felt, because Dex was carrying her up the stairs and toward the bright sunlight, the fresh air, toward safety.

He ran until they were several feet from the building, then gently lowered her to the ground. Brahern lay nearby, gripping his knee and whimpering.

Not bothering to ask what had happened, Sam stared up at Dex. She knew how she must look—her face covered in soot, her hair singed, her flesh and eyes probably cherry-red—but she didn't care. She was alive and Dex was here.

"Are you okay?" he asked, his beautiful eyes darkened with concern.

"I guess not if they sent the ME," she said, then coughed, long and painfully.

He didn't smile at her joke, barely paying attention to what she said as he examined her for injuries.

"Jesus," he muttered. He unwound Brahern's bandage, yanked off his shirt, and tied it around her leg.

He pulled out his cell phone and punished the keypad, calling 911 for an ambulance. When he hung up, he pointed accusingly at his Harley parked a few feet away.

"I can't take you to the hospital myself," he said in disgust. "Your car is all the way on the other side of the mall and all I have is that damned motorcycle."

"That's a *Harley*," she corrected, and it brought on another fit of coughing, but that was okay, because it made him smile and she got to see his dimples.

Then, she once again saw blackness.

****

Sam woke briefly and realized she was lying on something soft. She wanted to find out what it was because it felt so good, but she couldn't keep her eyes open. She loved this something soft, whatever it was. Before her eyes drifted shut, she noticed Dex sitting near her, looking worn out and worried.

"You're here," she whispered, even though it hurt to say it. It took her a moment to figure out she had a tube inserted in her throat.

A look of relief crossed his face and he straightened in his chair. "Yes, I'm here. I'm not leaving you."

"They always leave," she said on a sigh, then drifted away.

She woke up some time later and Dex was still in the room, but now he was pacing.

"Hey," she croaked.

She felt more like staying awake than she had before. She was still lying on something soft. She now knew it was a hospital bed. It wasn't as soft as she'd first thought, but compared to the cement of the mall's basement, it felt pretty damned good.

Dex rushed to her bedside. "How are you feeling?"

"Okay," Sam said. Her head, chest, and throat all hurt like a son of a bitch. Strangely, her leg didn't hurt at all. "How did you find me?"

"I knew something wasn't quite right by the way you acted, so I followed you."

"The way I acted?"

"Yeah, you were nice to me." He grinned and it made her heart do funny things. "I saw that you didn't go toward the police station, even though you said that was where you were heading, so I was suspicious. I almost lost you, but then I saw your car pull into the mall. By the time I was able to get there, I couldn't tell exactly where you'd gone. I cruised around until I saw Brahern come out of the building."

"Is he...?"

"He's in the county hospital."

"Hospital?"

"Yeah." Dex shrugged. "Hurt his leg. From what I understand, he's been confessing like a Catholic on crack since they brought him in."

"How long have I been out?"

"Only a day. You've actually been in and out. The fire was yesterday morning."

"Was anyone hurt?"

"No. There were a couple of security guards in the mall at the time. The fire was contained. Everyone's fine, thanks to you. The chief will probably want to give you an accommodation."

"If it weren't for you, it would be a posthumous one." Sam felt tears at the back of her throat as the reality of how close she came to dying sunk in. She let her eyes drift shut. "I'm glad I wasn't a bitch to you for once."

"Me, too," he said, squeezing her hand.

Eyes still closed, she said, "You didn't leave me."

"I told you I wouldn't."

Sam scowled, opening her eyes to look at him. "But, you...you're..."

113

"I'm what? An asshole like your husband? Look at the evidence, Detective. I'm not like him. Not like the other men you've known. When I say I won't leave, I mean it."

"But why?"

He shrugged. "I guess I've fallen in love with you. When I saw you lying at the bottom of the stairs, my heart nearly stopped. I was terrified."

A rush of emotion swept through her, hurting her throat, but in a good way this time. "You really mean that?"

"Hell, yeah, I thought you were dead."

"No, I meant the other part."

"About loving you?"

She nodded.

"Yes, I mean it. Why do you think I refused to have sex with you?" He grinned and the dimples creased his jaw. His eyes were tired and bloodshot, but they still sparkled.

She was happy, so happy, but she was also so very tired.

"I want to sleep for a little while," she said slowly, her eyes already closing again. "But when I wake up, I'm going to tell you I love you, too. Okay?"

"Okay," he said softly. "I'll be here."

And he was.

If you enjoyed Poetic Justice, you may also enjoy *Tears of the Wounded* by Alicia Dean. Here is a sneak peek...

Prologue

His hands, slick with perspiration, trembled as he reached for the ammonium nitrate. Sweat beaded his forehead and trickled into his eyes.

He stopped and took a deep, calming breath, trying to get his nerves under control.

Why should *he* be nervous? Teddy was the one who should be nervous.

Theodore William Garrett.

He knew a lot about Theodore. He'd studied him long enough. Theodore's father had given him the name because he was a baseball fanatic and Ted Williams was his favorite player of all time. Theodore's parents were both dead now, his mother from cancer and his father, a year later, from a heart attack.

Theodore married his high school sweetheart, Tara, and they had a child, Lindsey. Lindsey was now a motherless fourteen-year old. Theodore currently had a beautiful girlfriend, even prettier than his lovely, deceased wife.

Theodore always seemed to come out on top. But that was about to change.

He'd waited a long time to make Theodore pay.

Well, it wasn't like he'd been totally idle. He'd kind of screwed with him already. Like, that shit with his wife. Talk about fucking up somebody's day.

But, he'd more or less been picking on Theodore. Kind of like a bully on a playground who takes a smaller kid's lunch money. In truth, Theodore was the bully. Theodore had stolen much more than his lunch money.

He could have taken Theodore out years ago. But what do they say? Revenge is a dish best served cold?

Death would have been too quick, too easy. Almost merciful.

No, he had something much worse in mind for Mr. Theodore William Garrett. The woman and the child were the keys. They were pawns. Instruments. Spoils of war.

He would make Theodore sorry he'd ever been born and he wouldn't rest until he'd avenged her death.

Yes, that's it. *The Avenger*. He was The Avenger.

He bent over the tiny plastic case. The work was very tedious, very precise. But the object had to be small.

Another cliché came to mind.

Dynamite comes in small packages.

He laughed, his sweat drying in the cool air of the dimly lit room.

He was no longer nervous.

Chapter One

Abby Bishop lifted her face to the sky, reveling in the taste of salt water on her lips, the cool sea air blowing through her hair, and the warm sun caressing her skin.

"Male dolphins are called *bulls* and female dolphins are called *cows*," Abby told the six passengers of her Blue Harbor, Florida dolphin-watching excursion.

Abby's gaze drifted to the girl who sat in the seat next to her in the cockpit. Lindsey Garrett was pretty, with wide, hazel eyes and perfect skin, only slightly marred by adolescent acne. The teenager's long, dark hair was pulled back in a ponytail, but beyond that, Lindsey made no attempt to look fourteen. She wore a nose ring and flip flops, a tight pink spaghetti strap shirt, and booty shorts that showed her butt cheeks.

If she'd been Lindsey's mother, Abby never would have let her out of the house dressed like that. Abby knew Wil didn't like it, but he sometimes let it slide, and Abby was in no position to tell him how to dress his daughter.

Abby had been dating Wil for over a year but

had only recently met Lindsey. The girl didn't seem to like her much, so Abby was pleasantly surprised this morning when Wil called to say Lindsey wanted to come along on one of her tourist trips.

So far, the girl hadn't said a word and her expression hadn't changed from one of abject boredom.

Maybe it was because they hadn't spotted any dolphins yet. They didn't always, but Abby had about a ninety percent success rate and prayed this would be one of those times. She didn't want to acknowledge it, but she was trying to impress Wil's daughter. Trying to win Lindsey over.

"Dolphins can't live long out of water because their bodies overheat. They communicate via a series of—" Abby stopped, her breath stalling as she spotted them, about a hundred yards off the port side.

She did this for a living and had seen dolphins hundreds of times, but the sight never failed to leave her momentarily speechless. In a breathy voice, Abby said, "There." And pointed toward the beautiful creatures. Two of them broke the surface at that precise moment, perfectly in sync.

Oohs and aahs arose from the passengers, a couple with a ten-year-old son, and three young men who looked to be in their early twenties. But Lindsey didn't move, didn't respond. Her gaze flicked to the dolphins, then back to Abby.

"The sounds are a series of whistles and clicks called phonations," Abby went on, keeping the twenty-six foot Bayliner even with the dolphins without getting any closer. One of the most important aspects of her excursions was not disturbing or harming the creatures. "Dolphins use their flippers to make sharp turns and sudden stops."

Lindsey spoke up. "What about the mating rituals of the dolphin?"

Momentarily disconcerted, Abby cleared her throat, then said, "Well, their courtship sometimes involves bumping heads. Most of them mate in spring and early summer and—"

"My dad, like, has so many girlfriends it's insane," Lindsey interrupted. "I just wondered if dolphins were man whores, too."

Abby nearly gasped. Not so much at her words, but at the malevolence in the girl's eyes. Abby's face heated and she purposely avoided meeting the gazes of her other passengers.

"If you'll watch, the dolphins will periodically leap from the water, normally in twos, while those behind them swim just under the surface, then take their turns cresting the water," Abby continued, not responding to Lindsey. She wasn't sure what to say next. It was a good thing she had her spiel down pat, and an even better thing that Lindsey didn't speak again.

Abby didn't really think Wil had other girlfriends. He didn't seem the type to cheat and the two of them spent a great deal of time together. Even if he did date other women, it wouldn't be a big deal. She cared about him, but they weren't necessarily in a committed relationship.

What bothered Abby about Lindsey's comments was that the girl felt the need to make them, in front of others who might or might not guess Lindsey was talking about the man Abby was dating.

The intentional attempt to inflict pain, to cause conflict, was what troubled Abby. She'd seen enough conflict in her life, encountered all the trouble, all the violence and mayhem she cared to. She also didn't want to cause Lindsey problems. God knew, teenage girls had enough already. Especially Lindsey, having found her mother dead from a suicide four years earlier.

And, selfishly, Abby didn't want to deal with an

angry, resentful daughter fighting for her father's attention.

The remainder of the cruise was mostly silent with Lindsey casting smug glances at Abby.

When it was over, Abby guided the boat into its slip and helped the passengers disembark. As Lindsey passed by, she smiled at Abby and swiped her hands together, as if brushing off dirt.

To Abby, the gesture seemed to say, 'My work here is done'.

****

"Got a live one, wanna take it?" Sheriff Ray Roberts asked, stopping next to Wil's desk, his hands resting on his protruding stomach.

"You know I don't go out on calls anymore," Wil said.

"Not even for a gigantic set of silicone hooters?"

"Come again?"

"Marlo Swain called. Seems she was sunbathing and a couple of boys stole her top. I told her to stay like she was so we could recreate the scene."

Wil laughed and lifted his hands, miming a typing motion. "No longer my job description."

After his wife died, Wil had given up his job on the bomb squad of the Miami PD so his ten-year-old daughter wouldn't have to worry about losing another parent. He'd moved here to Blue Harbor and taken a job as a deputy where the worst crimes were—well—stolen bikini tops. When Lindsey's bad dreams and sleeplessness persisted, Wil switched to a desk job. With her father completely removed from the line of fire, Lindsey had slowly improved.

"Nothing but a desk jockey now?" Ray asked.

"I'm leaving the tough cases to the rest of you."

Ray snorted. "Don't remind me. How we gonna handle those big ole fake boobies?"

Marlo Swain was a widow who lived in Blue Harbor during the fall and winter months. Her wealthy husband had passed away a few years ago, leaving her well off and large-breasted.

"You seem pretty sure they're not real. You have firsthand knowledge?" Wil said, grinning as Ray's face reddened.

"They're about as real as Barry Bonds' home run record." The sheriff sighed and looked around the room. "Guess I'll have to send Lesli, since she's the only female. Ronald would be so embarrassed he'd have a coronary and Prescott would tamper with the evidence."

"I'm sure whoever you send is up to the challenge."

"Yeah, I know, I know. The only boobies you're interested in are Abby's. Bet those are real, huh?"

"Hey, watch it."

"Aw, come on. All I can do is talk about 'em. Give me something."

Wil shook his head. "You're nothing but a dirty old man. Your ass should have been in a sling a long time ago."

"Guess it's cause I look like goddamned Wilford Brimley," Ray grumbled.

This was true. With sparse hair and a mustache as white as a fish belly, round, gold-rimmed glasses, and cheeks that were perpetually rosy, he could pass for Wilford Brimley...or Santa Claus.

Wil's cell phone rang and he looked at the caller ID. Abby. Wil flipped open the phone and mouthed to Ray he needed to take the call and Ray wandered away.

"Can I see you today?" Abby asked.

"With or without clothing?"

She laughed, but it sounded forced. "With."

"Is something wrong?"

She was silent, then, "I just need to talk to you."

"Is everything okay with Lindsey?"

"Lindsey's fine. It's not about her."

"Want to come by the station? I'll be here

another hour or so."

"No."

Wil felt like an idiot. He'd momentarily forgotten Abby was as vehemently opposed to police work as Lindsey. Abby had been reluctant to even go out with him until he'd convinced her that the biggest danger he faced was carpal tunnel syndrome and paper cuts. He figured there was a story behind her fear, but she never talked about her past and he didn't push.

"Can't you tell me on the phone?" Wil asked.

Silence again. He heard her take a deep, shaky breath, like she was trying not to cry. "I didn't want to do it this way."

Wil had that panicky flutter in his chest he'd had the day Lindsey called him, crying hysterically, from her grandpa's cabin. He'd had it again the first few times Lindsey's screams woke him from a deep sleep.

"Abby? What's going on?"

"I can't see you anymore. I'm sorry. It's just not working out for me."

The panicky feeling traveled from his chest to his hairline. "Tell me what happened." His throat felt raw and tight.

"Nothing happened," she said wearily.

"You owe me an explanation." Now he was pissed. *Great, that's sure to change her mind.*

"There's no explanation to give you. I was reluctant to get involved with you in the first place, with anyone, for that matter. It's just been too much, too fast. I can't do this. I'm sorry. Goodbye, Wil."

"Abby?"

She was gone. Wil snapped his phone closed and looked around the room. Ray was talking to Lesli, no doubt sending her out on the call. Latham Prescott hovered nearby, gesturing with his hands. Wil figured he was trying to talk Ray into letting *him* go. Ronald was pouring a cup of coffee, probably relieved that whatever was going on didn't involve him.

No one was looking in his direction. Pressing his fingers against his closed eyes, Wil was relieved to find them dry...relieved he was only crying on the inside.

****

The bar was one of those out of the way places...dark, shabby, without the calypso music and island trappings of the other, more touristy establishments. Even its name was unpretentious, 'Jerry's'.

The Avenger scooped a handful of nuts from the bowl on the bar, fed them into his mouth via the opening between his thumb and index finger, then washed them down with a Samuel Adams.

Pulp Fiction played on the TV hanging behind the bar. "Can you switch that to the news?" the Avenger asked the bartender.

The guy was fat with a goatee and long gray hair tied back with a leather cord. He held up a chubby finger. "Hold on, pal."

Pal. He hated that. It had never bothered him until he heard a comedian on television say, to him, pal was the same as fuckface. He hadn't thought of it that way before. Now that he did, he couldn't stand it.

"Sorry," the bartender said, still holding up a finger. "Gotta see this part."

The movie was at the scene where Samuel L. Jackson quoted a bible scripture just before he blew some guys away. The bartender said it with him, word for word, ending with, "And you will know my name is the Lord when I lay my vengeance upon thee." He chuckled and shook his head. "Man, that Samuel L. Jackson is one badass son of a bitch."

No, motherfucker, I'm *a badass son of a bitch. Samuel L. Jackson is just playacting.*

The bartender picked up the remote. "Here's

your news, pal. Not a lot going on."

There sure wasn't. Not like there had been when he and Wil lived in Miami.

He watched the blonde anchorwoman drone on about the happenings, her expression never changing from wide-eyed delight whether she was talking about Jet Ski races or the war in Iraq. She was cute but sucked at reporting the news. Maybe she sucked at something else, and that was how she'd gotten the job.

A photo of Mayor Bingham flashed on the screen. Mayor Micah Bingham—former Miami Chief of Police, Wil's best friend, and the man who had condoned Wil's actions—was speaking in a public forum one week from today.

Vulnerable. Exposed.

He took another swig of the Sam Adams and gave a satisfied burp, wiping his mouth with the back of his hand.

The news just got interesting.

www.ingramcontent.com/pod-product-compliance
Lightning Source LLC
Chambersburg PA
CBHW072230190626
46809CB00017B/1673